4 7 55

Told in Confidence

Fiction

Among Women Only
The Beach and A Great Fire
The Comrade
The Devil in the Hills
Festival Night and Other Stories
The Harvesters
The House on the Hill
The Political Prisoner and The Beautiful Summer
Summer Storm and Other Stories

Non-Fiction

Dialogues with Leucò
A Mania for Solitude: Selected Poems
Selected Letters, 1924–1950
This Business of Living: A Diary, 1935–1950

Cesare Pavese

Told in Confidence
and other stories

EDITED, TRANSLATED FROM THE ITALIAN
AND WITH AN INTRODUCTION BY
A. E. MURCH

Peter Owen · London

ISBN 0 7206 0390 0

Translated from the Italian *Racconti: Pavese* and *Cesare Pavese, Racconti*

PETER OWEN LIMITED
12 Kendrick Mews Kendrick Place London SW7

First British Commonwealth edition 1971

Racconti: Pavese © 1960 Giulio Einaudi Editore S. p. A.
Cesare Pavese, Racconti © 1968 Giulio Einaudi Editore S. p. A.
English translation © 1971 A. E. Murch

Printed in Great Britain by
Bristol Typesetting Co Ltd Barton Manor Bristol

Contents

Introduction

Almost all Cesare Pavese's literary work (with the notable exception, to date, of his early essays on American and English writers) is already available in English translation : his *Selected Letters, 1924-1950* (Peter Owen, 1969), his diary, *This Business of Living* (Peter Owen, 1961), his poems and classical studies, nine of his novels and more than twenty short stories, collected in two volumes, *Festival Night* (Peter Owen, 1964) and *Summer Storm* (Peter Owen, 1966).

This further volume, compiled like the other two from manuscripts found in his room after his suicide in 1950, has a special interest in that these stories show Pavese's urge to broaden the scope of his literary work, his increasing preoccupation with psychology, his concentration on presenting, often at considerable length, the trains of thought passing through the minds of his main characters. Very understandably, most of them are written in the first person. Indeed, he gives singularly little attention to naming his characters, often indicating them in general terms—'The Captain', 'The Hermit', sometimes only by an initial. When he does give a name to his characters, he may change the spelling part of the way through. For example, the girl in 'Fag-End Blues' is called Daina, Dina, or Dinah.

In this group of stories Pavese's characteristic attitude of mind towards life in general is clearly revealed, his habit of morose introspection, his love for the hills and vineyards around the village of San Stefano Belbo, where he was born on September 9th 1908 and where he spent his boyhood, except for the periods when he attended school in Turin.

He identified himself to a considerable extent with the problems facing that farming community and admired their philosophical acceptance of such disasters as poor harvests, fire and floods. He was acutely conscious of his failure to conform to the accepted pattern of love between a man and a woman. His own experiences with women had been humiliating, crippling his self-respect. He longed to be loved, yet bitterly resented any attempt by a woman to 'mother' him. This is brought out very clearly in his story 'The End of August', when the central character says of his patient and loving mistress, 'Seeing her standing there, full of sympathy and affectionate understanding, was more than I could bear . . . and, for the first time, I hated Clara.' Pavese seems to take for granted that all women are faithless and immoral. In his diary (24th November 1949) he referred to a comment made to him by a literary friend : 'D. has remarked that my women are strumpets. She is amazed by it. My amazement is that it should be so. I have never thought of it.'

This particular collection of stories, written during 1940 and 1941, shows that at this period Pavese was experimenting with a view to broadening the background of his fiction. Hitherto, his work had been concerned with literary studies of English and American writers, reappraisal of Classical myths and legends, and fiction with a background of the Italian countryside, life in a busy northern city, generally Turin, and the diversions it offered to young people living there, such as dancing in the public parks, swimming or boating excursions on

the River Po. Pavese felt an urge to extend the background
of his fiction to include the sea, or at least the sea-shore,
and the fascination it exerted on the minds of young lads
who had never yet seen it. Pavese linked together a series
of stories and poems under the general title of *Caiu
Masino*. From this particular group I have selected two
stories : 'Fag-End Blues' and 'The Man They Sacked' to
include with Pavese's other outstanding tales.

These experimental tales differ so widely from one
another that it seems advisable to consider them indi-
vidually. In 'The House by the Sea', Pavese planned to
write under the feminine pen-name, 'Flora', attempting
to express the thoughts of a recently married bride about
her husband. Not surprisingly, the bride's trains of thought,
written in the first person, are not entirely convincing,
but her husband's views have a ring of truth in his
objection to her sunbathing in public and the embarrass-
ment he feels when he and his wife are surrounded on the
beach by a crowd of her young friends whom he does
not know. This fragment, written in January, 1940, may
well have been Pavese's first, tentative draft of material
to be used in his novel *La Spiaggia* (The Beach) published
a year later.

In 'The Captain', Pavese re-creates the tension of sub-
versive, anti-fascist meetings held in secret in Turin during
the war years, the mutual distrust between members of
the group, the clash of opinions between young, hot-head
enthusiasts and the more cautious views of older, more
experienced men. Pavese himself took little, if any, interest
in politics. But he had attended such meetings on the advice
of a friend, and felt it was only fair to hear both sides
of any argument. He had, however, written several articles
on freedom, published in the periodical *La Cultura*.

Though Pavese was concerned mainly with freedom of thought, particularly with a man's right to express his own views on literature, verbally or in print, his writings had attracted the attention of the Italian political police. When they found in his room a letter from a friend who was known as a leader of the Resistance movement, Pavese was arrested, convicted and sentenced to a year's preventive detention in an open prison at Brancaleone. He was released after ten months, but his imprisonment, unjust in his opinion, embittered his already morose view of life in general, and 'The Captain' was followed by his novel *The Political Prisoner* (Peter Owen, 2nd imp. 1969) and his short stories 'The Intruder' and 'Gaolbirds'.

'The End of August' gives an outline of Pavese's view of a typical love affair, not a brief, casual encounter but an association that continued through the summer holiday months of consecutive years. Writing in the first person, Pavese remarks, 'There is something in my recollections of childhood that cannot endure the carnal tenderness of any woman, not even Clara. . . . She was very much in love with me. I did not love her, but saw no need to tell her so.' This theme of a devoted woman deeply in love with a man who does not love her but is quite prepared to take advantage of all she can do for him, recurs several times in Pavese's fiction, notably in his short stories 'Suicides' and 'Wedding Trip'.

'Mister Peter' is to a large extent autobiographical, written in the first person by a young fellow whose life corresponds with Pavese's own. Both of them were only six years old when their fathers died; both were brought up by a very strict mother on whom they were financially dependent; both had poor health and the same moody and perverse temperament; both had a deep love for the country, yet longed to travel and see the world. Mr Peter himself seems largely fictional, symbolising adventure and the lure of far-away places.

The remaining stories in this selection, 'The Hermit', 'The Sea', 'Nudism' and 'Told in Confidence', are remarkable for their insight into child psychology and their reconstruction of the thoughts of a man trying to recapture his own childhood impressions and ambitions.

One thing at least links all these stories together, their vivid presentation of life in Northern Italy during the first half of the present century, sometimes in Turin itself, but more often in country districts. Here, closely observed, is the stark realism of existence in the agricultural regions of Italy at that time.

A. E. Murch

The House by the Sea

The expanse of rough sea outside our window freshened the whole room. I happened to wake at dawn, feeling rather restless, and turned my head on my pillow. For a moment I lay looking at the open window, then, as I remember, I smiled and lit a cigarette. There came a break in the storm-clouds, bringing me light enough to see that Andrea's place was empty. This was another thing in which he was like my father. If there was any dampness in the morning air he always woke before daybreak and couldn't stay in bed. He put it down to his nerves, but I think it was probably due to his need to be alone sometimes, a desire every man has in his very blood. He once told me it was out of consideration for me that he went off in this way, because of a remark I had made, saying the idea of anyone watching while I slept made me shudder.

No doubt he was enjoying a cigar in the garden — one of those tiny gardens one sees in the Riviera, just a tree enclosed by four walls. I could imagine him strolling about without his glasses, his face as placid and innocent as a child's. I knew that look well, for I had often seen him cupping a cigar or cigarette in his hand, muttering away to himself.

But no. In those days Andrea's love for me was still fresh and strong, and the fact that I had married him gave him a certain self-confidence. Not that our love was cooling off

— poor Andrea — but he had come to the conclusion that it would be best for me to love him as a daughter loves her father.

He became more shy than ever — an odd thing in a man as resolute and serious-minded as he was — and was considerate enough to leave me alone when he had one of his moods of deep depression and would walk about mumbling to himself. I'm sure he deliberately stopped making passionate love to me all the time. Don't we all need time for private meditation, to collect our thoughts and face our moment of truth? By now his feeling for me has changed as I really hoped it would, and become an affectionate interest felt by someone fully occupied with confidential business activities, quite content to leave other people to live as they like.

That morning in the little garden I'm sure he was completely happy, his mood soothed by the freshness of dawn, though the weather looked threatening. After working so hard all the week in the city he must have preferred this place to the torrid heat on the beach. Already, on our first night together, he had half-seriously objected to my sunburned skin, tanned, he said, from exposing myself to the gaze of the general public. He shook his head in disapproval and threatened to cut my allowance, but it was really all in fun and ended as such little quarrels always do. What he disliked most of all was to appear beside me on the beach, grumbling that he was boiling while I was roasting. Many friends of mine would cluster round us, voicing all the traditional congratulations to a newly married couple, with jokes in bad taste, vulgarities I didn't know how to counter, suggestive remarks that meant nothing to him and made him feel an outsider. . . .

The Captain

On certain quiet evenings I used to say goodnight to my girl-friend at the corner and go up those dark stairs. Half-way up I looked through a little window at the wide and empty sky. I didn't stop, but mentally sent it a friendly greeting, glad that its light could reach me even here. Then I knocked at the door. I realise now, from the swift sidelong glances of my host, that he was giving me much the same keen, fleeting attention that, a few moments earlier, I had paid to the sky. At the time I rashly assumed it would please him if I seemed a bit of a fool. We talked for a while, then little by little I let the conversation drop and the room grew as quiet as it had been when I arrived. The dark walls seemed endless, stretching away into the distance from the lighted corner where we were sitting. My host evidently found me a congenial companion, and when I left him an hour later he invited me to come again.

He was a big man, by no means old. His restrained yet emphatic gestures convinced me he came of country stock.

I didn't venture to tell him frankly, in plain terms, about the matter occupying my mind during the evenings we spent together. That would have been as pointless as enquiring whether he had a preference for a particular colour or perfume. Besides, I wanted him to discover for

himself that I have a puckish sense of humour, enough
at least to make him smile.

'What are the latest styles fashionable women are wearing now?' he once asked me. I raised my head and stared
at him in blank amazement. 'I mean,' he went on, 'do
current fashions appeal to young fellows like you?' As I
hesitated he added : 'Or do you and the lads you go about
with think all women dress alike?'

He was always coming out with unexpected remarks
like that. I went to see him fairly often, simply because
he lived over a large office block conveniently situated
on a corner near a bus-stop. The street door was never
shut, no matter what time of night it was. There wasn't
even a porter, as far as I know. The first time I went to
see him, sent by certain political friends of mine, instead
of responding to my remarks he remained silent. Sometimes, though, he would suddenly and unexpectedly rouse
himself and ask me some odd questions, answering them
himself and then listening without batting an eyelid to
anything I could tell him. The vast room was stuffy and
smelt of disuse. It had an air of haphazard untidiness, due
to so much empty space. Only in the corner where the
light stood could one get the impression of being in a
furnished room. The corner itself was formed by two
old armchairs and a bookcase crammed with papers. I
found it exciting to be on such intimate terms with him,
but I was also aware of a longing for fresh air and for
solitude to make plans for tomorrow, as one always does
when alone at night. That period of quiet meditation,
after being with other people, seemed to set a seal on my
own virility. The smile and the fatuous thoughts I gave
my host afforded me a keener appreciation of the contrast
between us, showing how humble I felt, listening to him.

One evening he asked me : 'Why do you like coming to see me instead of going out to have some fun?' I gave him a half-smile and he went on : 'When I was your age I was much more keen on having a good time.'

'There's plenty of time for things like that,' I replied.

'Why do you want to get mixed up in politics, anyway? It's not at all the kind of thing for you.'

I felt hurt, and paused a moment before telling him, somewhat uneasily, that I wanted to hear both sides, simply in order to reach my own conclusions. He did not raise the subject again, and when he showed me out that night he did not invite me to return. Perhaps it was only because I resented being snubbed like this (not for the first time), that I was so upset, but as usual, on thinking it over, I decided it was all my fault, though I still felt annoyed that the damned fellow had managed to fathom my secret.

Consequently I dashed round next day to see my girl. She thought I had forgotten her, and demanded to know why. Obviously I could not tell her the truth, so I had to put up with a good many embarrassing moments while she stormed at me, saying I was no good at anything at all.

A few evenings later I climbed those stairs again, perhaps from force of habit or because I was longing for another period of quiet meditation. The Captain, as we called him, opened the door to me himself in his normal, undemonstrative way, as if nothing had happened. 'We can't stay away from each other,' I said, jokingly, concealing my own pleasure at being there with him again, and murmuring something to the effect that I came to see him, not in any half-hearted way, but because I had a good deal to learn. He did not enquire what this might be, but remarked instead that a man must learn to be alone.

I protested that I was already living alone. He smiled again and leaned forward into the circle of light. 'You're too young for that,' he said. 'All you fellows are too young. You chatter too much. Social occasions always encourage you to talk nonsense.'

I had the impression that it was essential to have comrades, if anything was to be done, and I told him so. He made no reply to that, but went on : 'What do you imagine you can achieve by chattering?'

'I don't chatter, except when I'm with a woman,' I said. Our conversation lapsed into silence, as usual. I asked him what he had against me, but he just sat staring down at the table and did not look up. Inside myself I felt even happier than when I was with my girl, and was just about to say something to make him smile when he remarked : 'There's one good thing about prison. It teaches a man not to talk too much.'

'On the contrary, I believe he comes out with a great longing for company.'

'Certainly he does, for the first few times,' the Captain retorted. 'But then you realise he has learned to say less. The whole world becomes a prison to him, and prison is just what you young fellows need.'

At about this time our friend N. (one of the men who had advised me to contact the Captain), spoke of him with warm approval. Later, while discussing one of the Captain's projects, I asked N., at a convenient moment, what was his real opinion of him. He gave me a sidelong glance and heaved a sigh. I bluntly enquired what he had against him, and he explained that the Captain had lived in seclusion for so long that he had lost touch with reality and with current affairs. He had become a figure of the past, no longer capable of being our leader.

'He could still tell us what to do, though,' I said. N. gave me a dirty look. Later I talked to the Captain about him, but he seemed quite unconcerned and assured me that N. was a trustworthy young fellow. 'Is he any good?' I persisted. The Captain seemed rather annoyed by my question, and when I stopped talking he remarked : 'You're too intelligent! But don't withdraw from our organisation. Work for it.' I could hardly reveal what N. had said to me about him, so the subject was dropped. After all, there's more to do in the world than live alone in a garret. What I did with my friends was also important to me.

I felt annoyed, too, the next time we met. As I approached the house where I lived I noticed several pairs of eyes watching me from the window of my room. When I went in I found N. sitting in the middle of my humble apartment. Lifting his eyes from the review he was reading he gave me a casual nod. I had never heard him make a speech in public, for naturally he toned down his opinions when the Captain was listening. I stood in the middle of my room and enquired, with heavy sarcasm, whether I was disturbing anyone. 'Sit down and don't make a fuss,' N. said, so I stayed in the shadows, beyond the circle of light cast by the lamp, leaning against the back of an armchair, watching the Captain who came to sit opposite us. It seemed that they were expecting me to say something, but I had quite decided, since the case had thrust itself on me, to stay just beyond the lighted area and enjoy their discussions. Friend N. turned his head to stare closely at me, then asked : 'Have you quarrelled with your girl?' He meant to put me in a false position, for he knew perfectly well that every evening I left her at the usual time. 'Get on with your discussion,' I told him. 'I'm not with you at all.'

Each man picked out his own way of escape — the Captain chose his with complete composure, as if they were playing a game. N. turned his back on me as though I was, in very truth, not there. He stated his views with the utmost clarity. 'As I was telling you, Captain, Pippo loves being on guard duty. He can guard anything, no matter how dangerous, and nothing he sees can frighten him. But Pippo isn't here with us. For him, this is an undercover activity.'

'His day will come,' said the Captain quietly. Friend N. did not know that this was the very subject we had already discussed, and was amazed at our apparent indifference. But, knowing me as he did, he knew it was not the time to clash with me. He began talking calmly about his own plans, while I started walking round the room, pausing every now and then to judge the effect he was making on those present. To me they seemed more attentive than they usually were.

These were the very matters that N., only the day before, had said must be kept secret. Deep inside me I was glad to note he was following my own suggestions. I began walking silently up and down the room, on the lookout for any sign of dissension. The Captain scratched his eyebrows. 'Are you all agreed?' he asked sharply.

We didn't reply immediately, each of us waiting for someone else to speak first. Then I realised N. had already answered with an affirmative nod of his head.

'No,' I said coldly. 'Some of us, I for one, do not agree.'

'We know that,' N. retorted, 'and are glad you admit it.'

Then the Captain spoke, expressing his own views. He didn't enquire whether we thought our plan workable — that sort of project never is — but whether the various members had made up their minds to risk their own skins. Knowing us, he doubted it.

N. stated that in his opinion there was no difficulty whatever, as long as things were carried out as planned. I laughed, for I knew better than he did what the Captain thought about it all. There was no point in upsetting younger members. They would only get their fingers burned.

When N. had made his own opinions perfectly clear, the Captain shrugged and brought the debate to a conclusion by saying; 'Then everything has fallen through. Don't let it bother you any more. Just forget all about it.'

'You see,' N. said to me as we went down the stairs together, 'the Captain isn't really one of us. Have you made up your mind about him yet?'

'He's right, though,' I said, adding rather reluctantly, 'Only a very stupid man could still be in any doubt about the Captain's opinion of people who talk too freely.' 'Then it's up to us to show him we are not prone to gossip,' N. retorted.

In the ordinary way I'm a taciturn fellow, but I had spent the early part of the evening with my girl. Consequently I had been talkative, even aggressive, with members of the group. She and I, sitting together in a cheap coffee bar, had made certain promises to each other. Then we strolled through beds of spring flowers, perfectly happy.

My heart was light as I left the Captain. Now, walking with my friend up one avenue and down another, I could not bring myself to return to the meeting. The debates and the atmosphere of tension were just as they had been when I first went there.

N. and I were old friends and we often walked, side by side, without saying a word, each of us deep in his own thoughts, quite untroubled by the silence. On that particular evening I had nothing much in mind, enjoying my memories and savouring in advance so many debates that were still to come. N. seemed to me capable of doing everything, taking on everything, on that never-ending evening in March. I was young then.

'Poor little fellow,' said N. 'It troubles you.'

'Doesn't it trouble us all?' I retorted.

'What troubles me,' said N., 'is that he's worn out, shrivelled up.'

'He's worked harder than we have.'

'Actually, he's a dry old stick.'

'Don't tell him so,' I protested.

'I wonder if we'll be like him, one day.' He sighed, then added : 'If things go on as they are at present, I'm very much afraid we shall.'

The sun shone all day, and I can't tell you how much it pleased me. I was working that year — the first job I'd ever had. Every morning I went to the huge factory, brightly lit by wide glass windows. Beside one of those windows I worked as a designer and clarified my own ideas. Now and then I used to go down to a large room where certain employees were operating a row of machines. In passing, I winked at a tall, well-built young fellow who was operating a lathe. He was alert and observant.

A few words, all we had ever exchanged, gave me a hint
of his political views. As yet, we had not come to any
understanding, nor had we pledged ourselves to any
political group, but I was well aware that, had I wished,
I had enough excuse to talk to him. However, I was
putting off doing so, because, at bottom, I realised that
what counted was not any action we might take. What
mattered, at least to me, was to maintain our secret
understanding — something far more precious. It gave
me the feeling that, independent of myself and of my col-
leagues, reality itself was moving towards us.

My girl kept her promise. Consequently I went home
rather later than usual, completely exhausted and happy.
I no longer had any occasion to visit the Captain, but
I often thought of him, picturing him up in his room
alone and disconsolate, standing by the window that,
in this weather, had to be thrown open. N. told me that
someone or other still went to see him, for in his time he'd
enjoyed a lot of company. The few who had not gone
away still tried to help him.

In those days, N. rushed to and from our headquarters,
frantically occupied with setting up his Unions through-
out the province. He knew I disliked such organisa-
tions, so told me less and less about them. As luck would
have it, my own work kept me in town, otherwise I should
have felt obliged to go away myself. Such caution on the
part of N., who was no longer a boy, gave me some
anxiety. Between one trip and the next, N. became his
normal self again and would telephone about meetings he
had arranged, and what he had said about me at discussions in his own rooms. He replied to my objections by
pointing out that the police were too busy chasing a
phantom killer through the whole province to bother

about pecking around for clues in the city. For the moment he had put in my room certain items of information I already knew.

Striking a different note, he often reproved me for calling on the Captain when I had only just left my girl and was not in a fit state to be depended on. Losing patience, I retorted that he'd do better to keep a closer eye on the young fellows who were entertaining girls in his room. Politics and women don't mix.

One good thing between us, the only one, I think, was that I could tell him the truth to his face. On such occasions he adopted a serious air and explained his point. This time he stated that those girls of his were not women, but consciences. Like me, and like himself, they felt the need to take action. When his Unions knew how to wrestle with the problems facing them, who knows how many women, how many factory girls, they could organise.

I knew my friend very well and realised that the answers he gave me, smiling as he did so, were quite insincere — spoken from the teeth outwards. 'You called these women "consciences".' I muttered. 'Don't make me laugh!' However, the discussion was now open. N. insisted that the essential thing was to have the courage of one's own background.

'But I have no background,' I persisted. My friend laughed and asked me how I spent my evenings. 'Wandering round the streets,' I told him. 'Stop doing that. Stop it,' N. said. 'Even you have a job to do.'

Sometimes I grew irritable and tried to spend my time elsewhere. I took my girl out boating or if anyone telephoned me I made the excuse that we were going up the hill to enjoy a bottle of wine. Anything to avoid turning up at N.'s home in sheer desperation. We had nowhere else to go, and he was always willing to give us a hearing.

One day in the factory the fellow working the lathe gave me a furtive wink. He was ready to talk to me then and there, but it would not have been wise to enter into an argument, so he contented himself with staring, under my very eyes, at some huge lettering high up on the workshop wall. It was intended as a joke, but Severino (that was his name) gave a wry smile. As for talking with him, I had already given N. my word not to do so. That matter arose one day when I lost patience with N.'s sarcasms and told him my real job was working under water. Actually, I said it simply for something to say, but N., the devil, instead of laughing, took it very seriously and was most solicitous for my comfort, showing he believed me. His words were heard by two or three others, who passed on the information that this was my real job, and I quickly gained a reputation as a specialist in deep sea diving.

I decided not to sound out the lathe-operator at this stage. I preferred to watch his comings and goings, noting his sly management of a furtive cigarette, the conceited insolence he could convey by his very walk when he had to present himself to a superior. 'I wonder how he spends his evenings. Probably in making love, like me,' I thought to myself. His fellow workers understood the meaning of every glance he gave. I was glad to know that.

One day I accepted N.'s invitation to join him on one of his cycling expeditions. He wanted to trace a man who owed him a favour and might be able to settle a problem that was troubling him. Had he been unwise to trust a man who had carried out a certain investigation

for him? 'I don't think he can be a spy,' N. told me
naïvely. 'If he were, we should all have been arrested
by now.'

As we pedalled along, N. continued, as if to justify
himself, 'Sometimes it's essential, to get anything done, to
trust blindly the man selected for the job.' He remarked,
half jokingly, 'Mutual confidence is so important that,
like the crusaders, we should leave to God, or to the penal
code, the task of sorting out the saints from the sinners.'

'That's the Captain's opinion, too,' I told him. He gave
a half-smile at this, and I continued, 'He says,' I explained,
'that things are being carried to their limit. The more we
keep them bottled up inside us, the more revolutionary
does our movement become.' This time N.'s smile had a
certain air of tolerance. Then a turning in the road distracted his attention and we could no longer ride side
by side. I realised I was considerably concerned about
the way a spy carried out his duties.

The idea of prison, vague and adventuresome, took
hold of my imagination. What we were doing seemed to
me like a flight from something disgraceful, leaving a
bitter taste in my mouth. The presence of N. appeared
to be a tangible sign of something threatening. Our bicycle
tyres made a rustling sound over the wet asphalt and the
thought that this might be the last cycle ride I should ever
have, increased my tension.

'Who is this fellow you think might be a spy?' I asked
him suddenly. N. jumped from his machine beside an
empty bench on the avenue. He gave me no reply, but stood
looking around. There were a few low-built houses with
wooden roofs, no longer serving as homes for factory
workers, but still in use as holiday huts in an area already
absorbed by the city. One of these cabins had a door

standing open above the muddy step, and a sign-board showing it was an inn.

'Is this the place?' I asked him as we propped our bicycles up against a tree. Without any intention of satisfying my interest or curiosity, N. looked at me and said : 'The atmosphere here should please you.'

'Go on in, then, and be quick about it. I'll keep an eye on our bikes,' I said.

'If anyone comes along, don't take any notice,' N. sang out from the doorway.

I gave a shrug as I stood alone. Beyond the trees stretched a long meadow, uncultivated since it followed the boundary line. Farther off stood a few more isolated houses, all more or less alike and equally dull. After the rain, in the fresh sunshine, I thought to myself, 'One of those would just suit me.' I lit a cigarette, hoping to enjoy my thoughts in peace. The anxiety I had felt at first grew less, not that I had felt afraid, but because I so much disliked the idea of becoming too involved in those activities myself. We sometimes met by chance in the evening after supper, or as we arrived at the factory in the morning. I could wander about wherever I liked there, listening to discussions and hearing about all the little unforeseen things that happen every day. It struck me that, basically, having to stand guard over our bicycles was not very different from being in prison, except for the length of time it lasted. 'A man has to stop and think,' I said to myself. 'If he stops too often, it comes to the same thing.' It's a much more terrifying thought that perhaps a man is not allowed to smoke in prison. I'll ask the Captain, I decided, as soon as I have the time.

Naturally, I did have time. On the following afternoon, as I stood leaning against the Captain's window, I thought

over our escapade — for that's all it amounted to — and
the strict secrecy N. wanted me to observe with everybody. Going up to his apartment, I found another visitor
there, a Signora Bianca.

'Ah!' she exclaimed, 'you're a friend of Carlo's,' as soon
as she heard my name. Her own meant nothing to me.
There she sat, wrapped up in herself, sitting on the edge
of an armchair, looking from me to the Captain, with a
solicitude wholly maternal.

Before long the conversation lapsed, because I thought
the Captain would prefer me to say nothing at all. On the
other hand, the signora seemed to be involved in heaven
knows what pleasant anticipations. On several occasions
she began to hold forth on matters that not one of us
could understand. The Captain interposed his usual sarcasms and objections about people I knew. Eventually
the signora moved as if to rise from her chair. Looking
around the room, she said: 'There are still certain
things. . . .' The Captain searched through a cupboard
and brought back a packet about the size and shape of
an exercise book which she quickly slipped into her hand-
bag.

'One does as much as one can.' Her voice sounded
evasive as she rose to her feet.

When the Captain came back after conducting the
signora to the door, I was standing by the window, thinking more particularly about the excursion I had just had
with N. 'What have you got to smile about?' the Captain
asked me. 'Such silly things happen,' I replied. But the
Captain was in a bad humour. 'I hope I didn't disturb
you,' I said. 'Not at all,' he assured me, as he picked up
his hat. 'Shall we go out?'

Out in the street he broke the silence with a sigh.

'Why did you come to see me?' he said. He came to a halt half-way across the square.

'Have we offended the signora?' I said. He gave me a sidelong glance without batting an eyelid. . . .

The End of August

One night in August, the kind of night when the air is freshened by a warm wind that would soon become boisterous, Clara and I were strolling together along the pavement, exchanging a word now and then. To our surprise the wind caressed our faces, leaving on my cheeks and lips a sweet-smelling dampness and then going on to play with the dry leaves already fallen from the trees along the avenue. Looking back now, I don't know whether the warm emotion that came over me was inspired by the girl at my side or by the whirling leaves, but suddenly my heart overflowed with such a surge of feeling that I could not take another step, so I stood still.

Clara half-turned towards me and waited, rather expecting me to go on walking. As she turned, another gust of wind blew over us and without looking up she paused, as if expecting me to make her wait again. When we reached the heavy street door of the block of flats where she lived, she asked if I could give her a light, or would I prefer to go on walking. For a minute or two I stood still on the pavement, listening to the sound of a dried leaf being blown along the asphalt, then I told Clara to go along up. I would soon follow her.

A quarter of an hour later I joined her upstairs, sat down by the window, smoking and enjoying the scents brought to me by the wind. Clara called to me from the other room, asking if I was feeling better now. I called out to let her know I was waiting and a moment later she was standing close beside me in the dark room, leaning across my chair, sharing my enjoyment of the warm and gentle breeze but saying nothing.

All that summer we were almost completely happy. I cannot recall any quarrel between us. We used to spend long hours lying side by side before falling asleep. Clara understood it all and in those days she was very much in love with me. I did not love her, but saw no need to tell her so. Yet now I know this was the night when our happiness began to wane.

If only Clara had taken offence at my bad temper! If she hadn't been willing to wait for me so meekly! She could have asked what had come over me. She might have tried to guess it for herself, all the more so since she did not lack perception. Seeing her standing there, full of sympathy and affectionate understanding, was more than I could bear. I hate people who display such self-assurance and, for the first time, I hated Clara.

It so happened that the storm of wind in the night brought back to me, quite unexpectedly, a pleasure I had felt long ago. I was aware of it pricking under my skin and in my nostrils, one of those stark and secret memories our bodies can evoke, a store of recollections we regard as a natural development from childhood onwards.

The beach at the place where I was born is crowded in the summer with bathers and sunbathers roasting themselves in the sunshine. For three or four months of the year, life is full of variety and movement, as unsettling and disruptive as a journey by train or a removal to another house. Beach huts and footpaths swarmed with boys, family groups and half-nude women who no longer seemed women to me. They were simply bathers. The boys, though, had names, as I did. I made friends with them, took them out in a boat or ran off to play with them in the vineyards. The bathers' children wanted to stay by the sea from morning to night. I had a hard job persuading them to come and play behind the broken walls, on the hills or up the mountains. Between the mountains and the fields there were many villas and gardens. In the end of season storms, squalls would throw up masses of vegetable debris that looked as if flowers had been squashed against the stones.

Clara knows now that stormy winds in the night bring back to me memories of those days. She admires — or used to admire — me so much that she would smile and say nothing when she saw me overwhelmed by memories. If I talked to her about them, tried to share them with her, she would almost throw her arms around my neck. That's why she doesn't know that was the night I realised I hated her.

There is something in my recollections of childhood that cannot endure the carnal tenderness of any woman, not even Clara. The summers we spent together have taken on a colour, an atmosphere, of their own. Drowsy moments when a feeling or a word may unexpectedly rekindle the fire in memories we had forgotten. Instantly, distance means nothing. It seems incredible that such happiness can spring to life again from a period long past, almost lost in oblivion.

There was a boy (myself?) who used to stroll along the sea-shore at night, captivated by the music and the unrealistic lighting of the cafés, enjoying the wind, not the familiar wind from the sea, but an unexpected breeze

from the shore, bringing the perfume of flowers dried by
the sun, exotic, palpable. That boy could exist without
me, indeed he *did* exist without me, unaware that his
delight would bloom again after so many years, incred-
ibly, for someone else, a man.

But a man pre-supposes a woman, *the* woman; a man
knows all about a woman's body; a man should hold her
close, caress and embrace her. Any woman, for example
one of those who were dancing, so sunburned that their
skin looked black under the lights of the café overlooking
the sea. The man and the boy were strangers to each
other, seeking each other, living together without knowing
it, each conscious of his need to be alone.

Clara, poor girl, loved me very much that night. She
always did. Perhaps even more, for she, too, had her little
tricks. We sometimes managed to reinvoke between us
the mystery of lovemaking by pretending we were strangers
to each other, so avoiding monotony. But by this time
I could no longer forgive her for being a woman, one
capable of transmuting the far-away scent of the wind into
the smell of flesh.

B

Fag-End Blues

Masino — otherwise known as Tommaso Ferrero — had a job with a Turin newspaper that he found completely satisfying. In all fairness, though, I should add that it's easy enough to feel satisfied with working as a journalist at Masino's age — he was twenty-four or twenty-five — especially since he had a highly sensitive awareness of what would interest the public. I'm not talking now of his more intimate personal affairs — quite a different matter. Speaking generally, I should point out that his work as a reporter, a mild form of torture for any mentally active young man, left him almost the whole morning free for strolling round the town or staying indoors, working or idling the time away, and primarily to enjoy the spectacle of life as it wakes to a new day. I agree that Masino was one of those bright, dashing young fellows who, probably without even realising it, can create for themselves a magnificent way of living, full of adventure and a wide range of interests. The best of it is that, to do so, they have no need to go outside the great mechanical structure of life as it is today. In such a position, older, more experienced men would find that all they could do is to curse their lot and fret away their souls, mourning for bygone days. Instead, we newspaper men just adapt ourselves like a pendulum and keep happy. After all, that's the most important thing.

34

Masino, then, woke one morning full of energy and listened with profound complacency to the noise of trams and motor cars coming up to him through the open window, rising above the pungent fumes in the street to his room that until then was full of fresh air.

By this time, the people of the house were knocking at his door. They had taken it upon themselves to clean his room and make his bed *every morning*! After a brief exchange of greetings they clustered round him, pestering him to let them make a start. Being the kind of man he was, Masino yielded to this pressure, mentally linking his retreat with another great cosmic urge — a longing to plunge into water and try out his muscles. All the usual odds and ends of thought, impulses and ideas drifted through his mind, as they normally do in the morning. But there was something different about this particular day, something much more definite. Now and then Masino started to whistle, a sure sign that he was thinking out a way to make money. His plan was already clear in his head when, striding out briskly as if late for an urgent appointment, he swung through the doorway of his room, shouting to the whole house to let him get out and leave him in peace.

In due course there he was, back again, sitting at his little table in the freezing cold. The window was closed now, muffling the noise of the trams. A couple of books lay on the table, with a pile of printer's proofs, headed: Dramatic Performances and Stage Directions. Masino was smoking and thinking hard. He now knew exactly what he wanted to do. His idea, simple yet ambitious, was to write a happy song. Not for publication, nor to be circulated among his friends, but just to create a *canzonetta.* He felt a kind of physical necessity to satisfy this urge.

Masino was a bright lad and knew better than to imagine he could get up one morning and start writing poetry straight out of his head as if he were dashing off a thank-you letter. He already had a lyric in mind — a blend of adventure and lighthearted philosophy — but to bring these ideas to fruition is by no means easy and would be pointless anyway. No matter what Masino had in mind for his lyric, he had for some time been aware of a growing conviction (and was especially aware of it on that particular morning), that he was not the sort of man to live with a woman. This had nothing to do with having a wife and children, nor a mistress to waste his evenings with idle chatter and exchanging kisses. Masino knew what to do. Perhaps the root cause of his lack of interest was simply the fact that he viewed a lovely woman as someone to pass the time with, while the only woman who really matters to a man will bind him hand and foot. Then there's the nuisance of remaining faithful to her. Masino wanted nothing to do with that. Whether he was right or wrong in these ideas of his, in one respect they were well founded. He had never deceived himself about love. He was a cynic, as many people were after the war.

Masino had his own views about women. He was a native of Piedmont, and Piedmontese men keep themselves to themselves. Even now we don't know enough about them to understand. Their women folk must be either stupid or cunning. I can tell you that when a Piedmontese lad brings home a girl he wants to marry, the rest of the family at once do their best to drive her away by ridiculing her personally. So they lose her services which they could have had for nothing. That's the way things are in Piedmont.

Masino had not written a musical comedy since the war, because his ambition was to become known to the public as a more serious writer. The only thing he really loves is his birthplace, and he raises his glass to it every chance he gets.

To look at him, on the morning I'm talking about, sitting smoking in his room, humming to himself or whistling in his ear-splitting way, he certainly didn't seem to be harbouring a grudge against love, still less about life. Yet he had already written the title at the top of the first page : Fag-End Blues. 'Blues' means a melancholy song, as Masino knew well.

There he sat, smoking his last cigarette of the morning, gazing out of the window. The October mist had cleared by now, leaving a cloudless sky, bright and almost warm. On the table in front of him lay the theme song he had just finished for his blues. The refrain always has to be written first and Masino was enjoying giving it a final polish. Nothing is pleasanter than sitting smoking and revising one's practically finished work. Every now and then he glanced at it again. The words ran like this :

Throw away your fag-end. There are plenty more around.
Why stand staring down at it?
And if a faithless girl-friend plays you false,
Why worry? There are a hundred better ones around.
Cigarettes are to be used, then tossed aside.
It's the same with women. Don't wait to get your fingers
                                                                    burnt,
Or hang on to your fag-ends when there's nothing left to
                                                                    smoke.

By this time Masino's mood had changed. Now he felt an urge to move about, go somewhere, enjoy what life had to offer and express its significance in his *canzonetta*.

At last a thought struck him. At this time of day the Variety Café would be quiet. He could work there. He urgently needed a change of scene, so he quickly got ready, remembering vaguely that the café was a favourite haunt of singers and instrumentalists.

It's always easy enough to start anything, but bringing it to completion is the devil's own job, a maxim so well known that the mere mention of it seems too silly for words. That's what Masino had been trying to do, slaving away, cursing through his clenched teeth while his head felt fit to split, forcing himself to create, within the traditional limitation of a couplet, some story or other that could lead up to his *ritornello*.

There were no customers in the café just then. A white-coated bar attendant with a broad, wrinkled face was idly fiddling with the espresso coffee machine. Masino's brain was in such a whirl that he started humming over and over again the tune he had just written. Then he began talking to the attendant. 'How's the season going for you, this year?'

'The season? It doesn't make much difference to me. You're a song-writer, aren't you? Would you be willing to write songs in collaboration with another fellow?'

'That all depends.'

'Listen to me. I can put you in touch with a musician. . . . A fellow from the South, maybe even from Tripoli. His name's Ciccio, and he wants to have someone write a

great song for him. Somebody different from the ordinary
song-writer, you know, better educated. You seem to me
to be just the sort of man he wants. He's a well-known
musician and plays wind instruments. He's written a lot
of music, too. . . . I don't remember what.'

'Do you make a lot at it, working together?'

'If I had to live on that income I'd really be in a mess.'

'This Ciccio of yours, does he come from Naples?'

'Go and ask him. Here he comes.'

The bar attendant was an observant man who noticed
what anyone else might have missed — a gesture that
called him over to the little table where Masino was
sitting. Masino liked to be taken for an astute man of
business, and with an air of engaging frankness he made
a general comment or two. The barman did not reply and
went back behind the counter, pausing on the way to rub
a little tap with a duster he had in his hand. For a moment
Masino felt too embarrassed to speak. The barman said
no more and Masino hardly knew what to say himself.
Then, uncertain of his ground, he asked: 'Anything to do
with Ciccio's group in Naples?' The barman smiled but
didn't reply.

The huge fellow who had just come in had sharp eyes
almost buried in rolls of fat. He unbuttoned his long
coat, then, puffing and blowing, threw himself into a chair
at the first table he came to. 'Evening all,' he said.
'Good health, everybody. I'll have my usual.'

Masino looked at him with considerable interest while
the attendant worked the coffee machine. When the fat
man had been served with his coffee he started talking.
'It happens all the time. No matter where I go, I always
come across someone from Naples.'

'Sir,' said the barman, 'this is the gentleman I told you

about. He's a composer who can perhaps help you with the song you have in mind.'

The musician looked at Masino and said good-humouredly, 'As soon as I came through the door I knew he was the man. Well, my lad, you've something to tell me, I gather.'

Masino stayed where he was, thinking to himself : 'If I don't watch out he'll make me look a fool.' The attendant turned away towards the bar counter and Masino found himself agreeing with Ciccio in general terms that popular contemporary art in the form of *canzonette* might be of some interest to him.

'*Canzonette*? You must be joking,' the maestro replied. 'We don't bother to write words for songs. That's a purely commercial affair. What I'm looking for is someone, a poet, perhaps, who can write a superb song for me. An Italian song, of course. Are you a poet?'

'Yes, oh yes, but first we must reach a clear understanding as to the kind of song you have in mind. Words and music must be in complete accord, otherwise they can destroy each other, and the whole feeling of the song is lost.' Masino, trying to discuss the popular taste in music, felt he must sound an utter fool.

'What?' the fat man retorted. 'Of course I know the tune and the libretto must correspond, but they are two different things and can react against one another. Sentimentality, though, is concerned with only one thing, sentiment.'

'That's precisely what I had in mind,' Masino replied, irritated. 'We must have something modern that can express in popular form what people are thinking today. The music, too, must be in line with current trends.'

'I see what you mean,' the maestro declared thoughtfully. 'The song will not only be popular, it will also be artistic.' It might have been August from the way the maestro had to mop up his perspiration. Masino returned to his attack. 'Just as music has been brought up to date, the words must be those in current use today.'

'I'm not quite clear about that,' the maestro said, as if he was beginning to agree. Masino went on : 'The words are an embodiment of the tune, just as the music appeals to the soul. I'm thinking of words that correspond with the spirit of today's music.'

'A foxtrot is no longer romantic. Nor is a waltz or a blues. Take jazz, now. Have you written any words for a jazz tune? Who has the music score?'

Here Masino, shamefaced, had to confess he was new to the job. He half-feared a furious outburst. It did not come. Instead, the maestro was delighted. 'You're fine. Certainly I'm no budding poet myself. The tune for the song needs very sensitive handling.'

Masino, true son of Piedmont, leapt to the defence of jazz. 'In that matter we must learn from America. Have you ever listened to music composed for a film?'

'Don't talk to me about sound films. They're reducing our musicians to starvation. America? America? We're the ones who made America. We're all Naples men down there. What do you expect? We're the best in the world when it comes to composing melodies.'

Masino had it on the tip of his tongue to retort that Italy was not America, but he reflected that first of all he would be supplied with the tap-dancing rhythm or what passed for it. Gossip in the café suggested that even Turin wasn't certain how jazz would develop.

'In any case, sir, you'll want to see what I can do before you decide to work with me, won't you?'

'That's a good idea. Come and see me in my lodgings, though I haven't got a piano down there.'

'Yes, but I must prepare something for you, surely. What do you suggest?'

'My lad, if you want to work with me, the first thing you must have is inspiration. That's up to you. Do what you think best. Once I hear it and like it, then we can get down to business.'

'Maestro, you must give me an exhibition of your own musical skill, if we are to understand each other.'

'My music? I leave it all to a deputy, a man of straw. My real job is composing popular tunes. D'you know the successful "Our Very Own Tango"? That's one of mine.'

Early in the afternoon Masino was waiting at a street corner (an occupation he had not foreseen that morning), but one that had its part to play in the only adventure that had come his way that day. He had received a letter, ungrammatical but in a handwriting he knew, and he arrived promptly at the rendezvous specified in that letter. And here it's no good puzzling ourselves that Masino found it a bore to be going out with a pretty girl. Whatever kind of man he was, and no matter that he considered himself an enemy of all women, he could not resist the temptation to experiment and foster his very real hatred for them. It has been said that hate and love are akin, and in point of fact Masino, the champion, behaved as if he did not hate them at all. On that particular day Masino felt stupid and an arrant coward. Most men are a bit like that, and Masino certainly was.

The girl came along, only five minutes late. She was

fairly well dressed for a clerk, which she was. They
walked away together, he looking quite smart, she wearing a light brown coat and a little felt hat. As they met
they shook hands cordially.

'How are things going for you, baby?'

'O.K. I'm all right. Glad you could manage to come.'

'As you see.'

They sheltered under a porch, and Masino asked how
she had been able to get away at such short notice.

'I was all by myself and feeling lonely,' she said. 'There's
no one to keep an eye on us at the office. Thank you for
coming, darling.'

Masino very much disliked that mode of address and
had told her so several times, but the girl used it on purpose to tease him, smiling as she did so. This time Masino
decided to overlook it.

'Well, Daina, where shall we go?'

'I don't know. Anywhere you like.' She was called
Daina, but Masino made a practice of giving people
pet names, as a sign of possession, a word she could base
all sorts of fancies upon, when he was not with her. He
changed it from Daina to Dina then to Dinah, spelt the
English way. So much the better. One cannot always
succeed.

'It's odd, Daina, don't you think, that we meet only
once every now and then, for a day or two, and then go
for months without seeing one another again. D'you remember the last time? That meadow?'

Dina did remember. She bent her head with an uncertain smile and cuddled up closer to Masino's side.
'Let's go there,' she said to her companion. 'And that
time on the boat. Isn't that worth mentioning? On that
evening we nearly fell into the Po!'

After a short silence Masino came out with, 'Tell me then. What have you been doing to amuse yourself since we last met? All alone?' he added with a furtive little smile.

'Yes, I've been alone all the time. I hardly ever go out at all. Just once with that engineer, after that nothing.'

'You never really told me about that engineer, Daina. How did it turn out? All right?'

'How did you expect it to turn out? . . . Where are we going now?'

'I'm taking you to a fine place I know of, Daina. Shut your eyes and tell me about that engineer. . . .'

'Well then, he had a car. Once he made me get into it and took me for a ride to the hills.'

'And what did you do when you got there?' Masino enquired shrewdly. Actually, apart from sweet talk, there was nothing linking Masino and Daina except the memory of sexual intercourse once or twice, plus a little friendliness not clearly defined. But on this particular day Masino felt, as it were, a nostalgia for those brief experiences and wanted to hear all about that engineer, not out of jealousy but because it might be a good subject for starting a fierce argument later on. (Young people know all about that.)

Dina, very much surprised, told him : 'But it was nothing at all, dear.' Then, in a penitent tone, giving him a little smile, she went on : 'Not even what I did with you.'

'Thanks for telling me, Dina,' Masino started to say, but just then, as if to preserve his last shreds of dignity, a car almost knocked them down as they came out from the portico, and broke the thread of his thoughts.

Dina said to him : 'Truthfully, I was always left alone. Sometimes I cried about it.'

'Ho, Ho,' Masino laughed. 'You'd better find someone to marry you, my dear.'

For Dina this was no laughing matter. There was no one about in the street they were in at that moment, and Masino took advantage of the chance to give her a kiss, passionate but impersonal, caring nothing for the possibility that someone might come along. It was her spontaneous response to such kisses that had attracted Masino to her in the first place. He gave her another kiss or two, then they strolled on hand in hand. Dina paused a moment to shake out her coat, then gave a thought to her make-up. Masino held the mirror for her, realising that she was really upset.

'Who do you suggest I should marry? So far the men I've met have all been in a good position, you, for instance, and that engineer. I couldn't bring myself to live with anyone in my own class, so who can I marry?' She was speaking slowly, breaking off to powder her face and touch-up her lips. She sounded annoyed, rather than sorry, as she went on, 'So who can I marry? A workman? A labourer? A bricklayer? Then what? What sort of life should I have? I couldn't live with a factory-hand, either. He might knock me about. We'd never get on together. I simply couldn't.'

'I didn't suggest you should marry a workman,' Masino just managed to get a word in. 'The world's full of people. You never know who you might come across.' Without getting involved himself, Masino wanted his words to convey a certain meaning, but felt he was making a fool of himself. The fine self-confidence he had been conscious of at the start of the afternoon had vanished. Without realising it, Dina gave him a lead. 'I want to tell you something that happened to me. I've never said a word about it before. You know the fellow who waved at me, that Sunday when you took me out in a boat? He has a friend with piles of money, and another pal like himself. They go everywhere together and get up to all sorts of tricks. I happened to meet them in the street one day and the four of us went to a café. One of the fellows kept talking to the millionaire and the other told me their friend was frightfully rich, but a fool who had never yet made love to a woman. He suggested that if I were to fall in love with him it would be a fine thing for the three of us. Then they invited me up to their bachelor flat. The rich man came close behind me but he was too shy to say a word.

'The other two were busy around the flat, arranging everything, offering us tea and pastries. I chattered away, laughing gaily. After a while the fellow we saw in the boat started throwing his arms around me and kissing me. He wanted to undress me, but I wouldn't let him. Then two of them tried to persuade me and began threatening me. The rich one said nothing, so I ran over to him for protection, acting like a very determined woman, so he let me go.

'Well, I saw the other two men one day and they tried to walk along beside me, to keep me company they said. I didn't want them so they called me a fool. After all, I could just as well have got the millionaire to marry me, couldn't I? I could marry if I wanted to, but I don't. I was thinking if only I could find the right man. . . .'

Masino was listening. He wouldn't have wanted to say so, but the idea of Dina being made to strip in that room upset him for the moment and he tried to put his feeling into words : 'They are nothing but a couple of dangerous rogues, stupid too. That's no way to behave, Dina, is it?' he said with a smile. 'But getting a bit of fun out of life is a different matter. Don't you agree?' He tried to smile at her again.

Dina smiled in response, but she looked pale and clung more closely to his arm. Neither spoke for a little while as they stood in a close embrace.

'Come with me tonight, Dina. Will you? I know a fine place to take you.'

'Where?'

Masino tried to find the right words. 'Let's have a while alone together. You'd like that, wouldn't you? Just like that time in the boat.' He hugged her even more tightly.

'Not today, Masino. I don't want to. Let's go somewhere together. Let's go to the cinema.'

'Why? We haven't seen each other for such a long time. Come on.'

'No, Masino. I don't want to. Let's behave ourselves.'

'Why? Is there any reason why not?' His smile had a double meaning.

'No. There's nothing to stop us. It's just that I'm not in the mood. Let's have a long chat instead. It's ages since we've seen each other.'

'We can talk there. We'd be quite alone together.'

'Afterwards we mightn't meet again for a long time. It's no good, not today.'

'Come on, Dina. Be a good sport. Come along.'

'No, Masino.' Her voice was firm now. 'I'd rather go home right away.'

Masino had to accept the fact that there was nothing doing, that day. Dina was determined to be let off. His anger almost choked him but he managed to control it. Earlier, on his way to meet her, he considered making love to her as a matter of no importance, but by now his

desires had multiplied. She had turned him down out of
caprice. Simply a caprice. It annoyed him.

'Go home, then,' he retorted, starting to walk away.
'Go and find some other man to screw you.'

For a moment Dina stood perfectly still, then gave a
sigh that was almost a groan and walked away so quickly
she was almost running.

Masino had written his verses and was now sitting in the
café smoking and waiting for Ciccio. By now the maestro
had agreed, after a good deal of argument, to accept
Masino's suggestion of using modern language in his
canzonette, his blues. His fixed idea of what a song should
be turned out to be merely a fixed idea that had entered
his sensitive spirit to set right the evils of life in
general.

With his masterpiece in his pocket, Masino sat there
waiting. Meanwhile his verses were running through his
mind as if they were spoken aloud. The first one was
pretty well typical of all the others.

Fag-End Blues
How many pretty young girls you see in the street
Who look like dreams of love.
But if, poor fool, you stop one of them
You'll soon get wind of her.

You can watch them, models of propriety,
So shy they run away around a corner
If a man so much as winks at them.
Almost before they start talking familiarly

They'll ask you, 'Give me a fag'.
Then follows the usual rigmarole you know about.
But to go through it all a second time,
That would be a crime.

Women are made that way. It can be delightful
To smoke a cigarette with one of them, kiss her on the lips
Or lower down. But soon you'll feel uneasy.
Push her away quickly.

Like a half-smoked fag-end, such women
Emit a beastly smell.
Be careful, then, for charity's sweet sake,
And do not fool yourself that this is love.

Masino had managed to get that far. At last the maestro
came in. The two men greeted each other and began
walking towards the private rooms.

'Well, my fine lad, have you been working?' Don Ciccio
asked, seeing that Masino was feeling too embarrassed to
speak first.

'I've had a go at the blues,' Masino replied, taking the
sheet out of his pocket.

'We'll have a look at it later, later,' Ciccio told him.
'On the piano. Even a blues can be a suitable matter for
artistry. We're practically there.'

God willing, they arrived and climbed the almost impossible stairs and finally found themselves in a large
cold room full of a medley of unrelated objects. There was
a bed, a pair of trousers hanging in mid air, a guitar on
the wall, and mountains of musical scores everywhere.
There were a few oleographs around the guitar.

'Make yourself comfortable,' the maestro began. 'It's
rather chilly here in the afternoons.' Without saying more

he sat down at the piano, puffing and blowing. 'Now then,' he went on, 'is your *canzonetta* ready? Give it to me. If it inspires me, the matter is settled.' He took the sheet Masino passed to him (rather nervously, to tell the truth). Don Ciccio turned towards the music-rest, put down the manuscript and looked at the keys. Then he began : ' "Fag-End Blues"? Isn't that a trifle grotesque for a title? Oh, well, even the grotesque has some value. Now we'll see.' He read it through impassively, touching the piano keys now and then. Once, at the start of the second verse there was a crease in the paper, and he called Masino over to decipher a blot. Masino was calmer now and master of himself. When he had read the lyric, Don Ciccio looked at the keys again and began to play a tarantella, completely absorbed in it.

'I intended this for a blues tune,' Masino interrupted, somewhat timidly.

'I know you did, of course,' said the other. 'But just now I'm thinking about the plot. It gives me the idea that the grotesque element may not be too strong. What's your opinion, my lad?'

Masino, thus taken unawares, hardly knew what to say. There was a short silence, then Ciccio went on : 'It's verging on the comic. You've worked well, my lad, but we'll have to change the idea. The public won't put up with this, you know. We're saying the woman is a serpent, she's poison, and so far that's allowed. You're quite right, you know, lad. She's treacherous. You can't believe a word she says, but all the men are chasing her. No husband or lover in the theatre would quarrel with that. I agree with you, you know. . . . I'm not married. Picking up a woman is worse than picking up a cigarette end in the street. All she wants is money. . . .'

By now Masino had lost all hope but still wanted to interrupt the maestro, even with a lie. 'That's just the point. We're talking of street women.'

'Really? In this? That's yes and no, my boy. A blues song must be sad. All women can make a man sad. We can call them serpents, poisoners and so on, but we can't say that about street-walkers, my lad. Believe me, it simply can't be done.'

Masino, as we know, was humble by nature and a native of Piedmont too. He hadn't been bored by it all. He put his manuscript away with a philosophic air and stood up to go, but the maestro detained him to listen to a song he had written. It was supper time before he got away.

Masino was a conscientious fellow, and on his way home he thought over what he had written. Turning those lines over in his mind for the rest of the evening and all night, they now seemed to him worse and worse. He felt quite ashamed of having written them. Then he remembered how Dina had looked at him that afternoon, as though her very life depended on him. 'However could I have treated her like that,' he asked himself, a pointless question. Next morning Masino woke up and started working again, listening happily to the noise of the trams and motor cars in the street outside.

The Man They Sacked

Giantommaso Delmastro (the canteen cook at Lingotto's always called him Masin) was a good mechanic by the time he was twenty. When he was called up he was considered rather wild, but quick-thinking intelligent men always reveal their quality, and when he left the service, bored to death with it, he was a fully qualified motor mechanic with a certificate from the training school at Naples. His position allowed him to spend most of his time out of doors and gave him the right to argue with non-commissioned officers if necessary. So he went back to Turin, full of energy, and got a job with the Fiat firm, testing cars and motor-bikes. He began to think about getting on in the world.

He wanted to gain a diploma, and after spending all day rushing round the hills wearing bright colours, splattered with mud and blown about by the wind, he spent his evenings in a drowsy class of twenty men or so who had been working indoors all day. They acquired a great mass of useless information and a small amount of practical mechanics. After two years of that work he could pass an exam that would put him well ahead on the manufacturing side.

It seemed to Masin he'd achieved nothing at all. He remembered all the pretentious emptiness of army life, the time when they all had to work very hard to repair an

old shanty that would never be any different and that
nobody would look at anyway. That's what the world is
like, so let's close our eyes to it and take a diploma. So
Masin came down from the hills where he had been testing
engines all day, riding through the streets at breakneck
speed, drenched with rain and dried by the sun. What
he studied at night-school were the very things he'd been
practising all day. Knowing how to clean and reassemble
the engine that had been pulsating under him all day
while testing performance on speed trials, gave him satisfaction and a feeling of discovery.

That was not the only thing he learned at his evening
classes. He needed to improve himself, work his way
up. They showed him that all his life so far had been
concerned with material things. The houses he had lived
in were all filthy hovels. Masin had always known this,
and that as a boy he had always been hungry.

But materialism was a vulgar word, and Masin didn't
think of applying it to his memories of a year ago. He
absorbed it all like some heady drink, recalling the guitar
players in the pub, bloodcurdling threats uttered through
clenched teeth on street corners. His experiences as a
soldier were even more materialistic. He had always taken
life very seriously.

To cut the story short, his teachers at night-school
wanted him to learn he was an Italian. So were Julius
Caesar, Balilla and Cavour, who had all written in Italian.
There was Dante's *Divina Commedia* and works by Vin-
cenzo Monti. . . . An emigrant's chief treasures were his
country and his native language. It was Rome that brought
civilised life to the world. Only slightly less important
was the study of natural history. It seemed that such
material considerations existed so that a student could

emerge as a man. Masin had known many men in his
early days and later in the army. These were people
who could be relied upon, well-balanced men whose words
and deeds inspired trust, even if they were ruffians or
corporals. Masin himself could never think about it without being conscious of his manhood.

By now he had convinced himself that the silly old fool
who taught botany and wore a chestnut-brown suit,
stammered all the time and could reel off classifications
like a set of rules, must have played a part in helping
Masin to become a man. At the very least he gave Masin
someone to laugh at. The teacher of Italian Language
and History was a young married man, who read aloud
in an agitated voice and took far too much interest in
his students' private affairs, ostensibly in order to help
them enter the world of culture. He gave Masin someone
to curse.

One evening this teacher came in looking severe as
usual, striding forward to his desk, a rickety little table.
From it he took a pile of completed work written on the
scruffiest scraps of paper in the world — pages torn from
exercise books or old registers, blank bits cut from news-
papers, pages to hand in and have back. He placed the
pile in front of him, looked slowly along the class with an
air of cunning, then he said to the nearest pupil, 'Give
these out.'

When the sheets were all distributed a brief silence fell.
Then Masin half rose to his feet and looked at the teacher.
'What about mine?' he asked.

'Yours, Delmastro, is here,' the teacher replied, holding up a page he had kept back. Then, banging his hand
on the table once or twice, he went on : 'Delmastro, you
have written one of your usual essays. Last time it was

about the Church, now it is Pietro Micca. Will you explain to me how you could ever have written a thing like this?'

Masin found himself in some difficulty. He had felt a certain apprehension about it. Now his mind was at ease, though he didn't know what to say. 'I mislaid the theme and didn't know . . . it seemed to me. . . .' To himself he thought: 'To the devil with the silly old fool. What's the point of all this fault-finding?'

The teacher cut him short. He had already planned what he was going to say. 'I've already told you, Delmastro, that you could achieve a great deal. You're full of ideas, confused but lively. What you must do is free yourself from prejudice and read anything you can lay your hands on. The other time you railed at me about the Church. Where did you get the idea you had any right to air your views? Taking a general view, this is no longer the time to get on the wrong side of the priests. What do you know about them, anyway? Their interests lie in other problems, and they are particularly concerned with our Italian workers.' The young husband let himself go on the subject of the workers. 'Have you ever seen a blast furnace . . .? The State, the family and co-operation, these are our problems, as they are the eternal problems of all mankind. Now, you have given me an interpretation of the "Legend of Pietro Micca". Who says it's a legend? His whole personality is certainly brilliant, so much so that it's worth taking the trouble to discuss it. To amuse your fellow students we will read it aloud, but see to it that this behaviour does not occur again. Because,' he added with a little smile, 'certain historical studies can be dangerous.'

Masin was boiling with rage. His composition had been written on a suitable historical subject. Taking one thing with another he felt his spirit rising to defend his choice against the whole world.

'Will you come up to the desk then, Delmastro, and give your fellow students a short history lesson?' the professor suggested, still with his sarcastic little smile.

Masin walked over to the desk, giving the professor a dirty look. Then he picked up his page and began to read:

'The title is: "Discuss the heroic deed of Pietro Micca, his attitude towards his fellow-men and the idealism of his sacrifice".'

The apathetic students wriggled about for a minute or two before settling down to listen. One of them gave Masin a word of encouragement, and was instantly silenced by the teacher, who went on to say, 'Come along, then, Delmastro. Read us the whole of your text and don't forget the errors I have corrected.'

Masin began reading:

Pietro Micca was a hero of 1706, when the men of Turin were defending themselves against King Vittorio Amadeo III. One night, when the whole city was unluckily asleep, the French army was trying to burrow under the subterranean walls to get to the places where gunpowder was stored. One of the defenders, named Pietro Micca of Biella, stood straining his ears to catch a sound he thought he had heard earlier. He decided it must be coming from the canteen and sent a soldier there to fetch him something to drink, to pass the time.

The whole company was drinking there, preparing to escape. They urged Pietro Micca to come with them but he replied that they were all on sentry guard and must not leave their posts. He said to them, as he had often said before: 'Look alive, my lads. Our country is in danger.' But he did not know that all the men were terrified. When he had finished drinking from the cask they had all fled. So Pietro Micca remained on the alert, thinking of his country and that the drink he had just had would be the last he would ever swallow. Then he lit the fuse of a mine. There was a great burst of flame that spread along the corridor. So his country was saved and the ruins are still to be seen, until a statue can be erected to his memory in the piazza, showing the hero and the cask he drank from just before he died.

Masin read the final words almost scornfully and his hearers could hardly understand them. The class, hitherto held in suspense, began a continuous uproar, undeterred by whistling and calls for silence and the banging of hands on the desk, but finally came to order. There had been raised voices, a shuffling of feet, laughter, the devil's own row. The professor waved his hands in the air to induce calm, though he was smiling himself. 'It's nothing. They've heard it all, haven't they? Silence! Don't quibble over the style Delmastro has used, though it's not perfect. You see what his comrades thought of Pietro Micca.'

A voice from the back benches shouted, in the Piedmont dialect, 'Can't you see he's making fun of you?' The young husband stopped. He understood Piedmontese and the phrase had taken him unawares. 'Silence!' he said again. Then he turned to Masin, looking scared. 'What did you say? Is that true?'

Masin was saying to himself: 'What a fool! What an utter fool!' Then he went on, aloud: 'It depends on how you take it, whether you understand it. Sometimes a man studies so hard that he no longer realises what's going on around him. I once knew a department head who studied too hard. Anybody could fool him!'

Another outburst of scornful laughter came from the back benches, insolent and sharp as nitrate. The professor was trying to get away before losing the last shreds of authority. 'You confess, then,' he said, 'that you deliberately played a silly trick on us all?'

'What else did you think it was?' Masin could not refrain from asking.

'Very well, then. Go and report all this to the headmaster. Tell him, too, that I'll never admit you to any class of mine again. . . .'

As Masin walked out, one of the students tried to give him a surreptitious handshake Masin did not want.

Next morning, before it was really light, Masin was already out testing a motor cycle on the steep slopes of the Pino. He was taking a difficult meandering course that led him up among the vineyards and the trees. He liked riding through them, taking note of signposts and private boundary marks. Behind him, down there in the valley, lay Turin.

Not that Masin was paying much attention to the engine or to the track he was following. His eyes looked desperately tired, his headlamp had gone out. He took the sharp corners as if he was half asleep. His mouth was very sore from the drinks he had taken the night before. He had a violent headache that, in the stillness around him, seemed to be throbbing in time with the beat of his engine.

Masin was thinking of nothing in particular. His eyes were almost shut as he concentrated on getting down to the Pino, dismounting there and finding something to eat. Luckily it all turned out that way. He was on the final stretch of the track now, planing down from the crest of the hill to the level ground below. He cursed the turbine engine of a mechanical harvester that forced him to pull into the side of the lane. Then he was on level ground. There was no one to be seen in the village at this time of the morning.

He looked out for the café where he normally took a break. It stood on the road into the village from the west, close to the huge yellow posters facing the road, advertising Atlantic Oil and Spidolèine. There was a little girl taking down the shutters, just as usual. He gave her a sketchy salute, then went inside, where he found a pleasant warmth, like staying in bed at dawn. He sat down on a bench and did not move again until a fried meal was set before him.

The air was brighter now. A second customer came in, an elderly farm labourer with grey whiskers. His hand was shaking as he lifted his drink to his lips. Masin was chewing a piece of salame, somewhat disturbed by the presence of the other customer sitting there drinking. When Masin had finished his meal he rolled himself a cigarette and give a wide yawn. As the smoke drifted around him he started thinking. He certainly had something to think about. For one thing he'd have to get a lot more mileage on the speedometer. A visit to Villafranca, perhaps. With any luck he could get a good lunch there. He found this idea comforting.

He had nothing to do that afternoon. Nothing in the evening, either, now he'd been turned out of his night-school. So what? There were always vineyards needing helpers. Good luck to them! As for that teacher and his students they were all fools together, utter fools.

There was nothing especially interesting in his technical work, either. Did he want to spend the rest of his life testing motor cycle engines? Masin felt disheartened as he left the café and seated himself on the high extra saddle concealed on the machine. Glancing down he noted the long bare wiring of the electric system, the various attachments all visible and covered with dust, all in good order, all vital to the speed of the machine. He started off, his engine roaring, making for Chieri and the east where the clouds were glowing red.

Masin was very much aware of the stones thrown up against his shoulders by the speed of his machine on the rough track, and wished he could take a short cut between the houses. As he left the place he found himself on the straight descent road and covered that stretch like a breath of wind. Now he shot forward into the last lap, facing the rising sun, red and dazzling. By this time Masin's head was splitting.

At that moment he heard a cry, followed by a slight bump. He wasn't sure what to do, but he switched off his engine and dismounted. Two men were running towards him, shouting. Masin's knees were shaking. He had knocked down and run over somebody.

The whole affair was soon over. The authorities took away his licence, issuing a permit instead allowing him to take up factory work. He could well have been sent to prison, but was treated more leniently because the man he had killed was drunk. He was the farm labourer Masin had seen drinking in the café.

Masin had no friend in Turin, nor for that matter, in

the whole world. One fine day he jumped onto a train with 40 lire in his pocket, over and above the price of his ticket.

The Hermit

Nino was a spiteful boy — so I had always believed —
but now I realised that the mischievous tricks he played
were not due to caprice, at least no more so than pranks
I had played myself. I began to understand that the
house did not mean the same to him as it did to me. The
passage running through it from front to back, from
the street door to the garden entrance, filling it with a
green light whenever anyone came in, was for him an
assurance of freedom, recalling him to the open air. For
me, it was just the background for my hardened bitterness. There were rooms, one at least, always shut, and
if my sister-in-law opened it to clean and tidy it, Nino
always poked his nose inside. Then I felt a twinge of
annoyance, because I understood that for him the cur-
tains, the dressing-table, the chest of drawers, remained
in his mind only as a lovely, strange background to his
wild fantasies.

After my wife died I did not think I could still go on
living in that house. However I had gone back there,
with Nino, when July was at its height. During our
first days there, Nino never stopped bemoaning the fact
that we had left the sea behind us. That year, for the
first time in his life, he had come to know what the
sea was like, and he hadn't got on with it very well. He

looked like his mother, who in her last days had circles under her eyes and was obstinately set on eating the fruit she had liked as a child. Nino tried desperately to hide from me the sea-sickness, vomiting and fainting fits caused by the sea air. He was twelve and it didn't seem right for him to play all day in the water with boys of his own age. When I told him that we should inevitably be parted, he replied : 'You'll see, it will be worse than ever in that house now.'

He soon got used to the water and seemed more at ease, and was delighted when I let him go bathing in the river. But he would not go alone. Indeed I forbade him to do so. I went with him myself and Nino was sensible enough not to try to slip away. Possibly he realised that if he did he would be forbidden to go bathing again.

While by the sea he had made many friends, but here in the country he wouldn't go round with the bigger lads, nor with the few boys who lived in our street. He sometimes joined in their games, but never brought one of them home. From his earliest days here he was careful not to talk too warmly of his memories of the sea. He spent the morning in the fields behind the house or strolling round the noisy market among the market women and the peasants. He specially enjoyed watching the stall-holders and seeing the yokels being fooled by charlatans from beyond the hills, past the terraces by the river. They spoke with such vivacity, wore wide red cloaks and sometimes boasted of their travels in exotic lands. I still remember how excited he was when he got to know Colino, the fish vendor who kept a barrel of anchovies and travelled every year to Spain, to fill it again.

He was full of enthusiasm as he talked about it all at table. My sister-in-law — a good woman who had never left the district where she lived — made fun of him. Nino gave her a glare of hatred. Half-way through the afternoon we took to the fields, Nino and I, on our way to have a swim, he running ahead of me. The river was very wide at that point, out of all proportion to the banks where orchards and gardens sloped down to the water's edge, but it was not very deep. We waded across, undressed among the willows and lay sunbathing on a gravel bank. Then we plunged into a little lake near the far bank, and sometimes, out of curiosity, pushed our way through the thickets that grew, undisturbed, to the foot of the hill. Nino was extremely proud of his suntanned skin.

The first time I heard the hermit mentioned was at table. A word from Nino made my sister-in-law retort: 'He's a filthy fellow. All the women making a set at him couldn't manage to wash him clean.'

Nino replied that on that morning the hermit had appeared in the market, selling rabbit skins.

'Who is he?' I asked.

It seemed he was a young man who, fed up with working, had settled himself half-way up the hill by the river. He had excavated a kind of grotto. He kept a goat and allowed himself to be visited by devout people. The priest from the pulpit had already warned women against having anything to do with him, said my sister-in-law. Without looking at her, Nino said the hermit had a blond beard, a coat of skins and sandals.

'He's a heretic,' said my sister-in-law. I laughingly made a comment that in all probability he was just a layabout. Nino choked as he explained that before becoming a hermit the fellow had been a sailor and had travelled all round the world. Once he had been rich, but had given

all his money away, as everybody knew — Colino, for
example.

'Stop saying things like that,' I shouted at my sister-in-
law, who was laughing. 'You're just a stuck-up fool!'

That afternoon we didn't go bathing. Nino (who never
cried when he was punished) disappeared through the
garden door. Towards evening I went out in the street
to look for him. Some workmen were starting to build a
new church in the country just beyond the village and
all the village boys were standing around watching them,
but nobody had seen Nino. At last I went home again
for my supper and found my sister-in-law bringing him
in from the garden. That's where he had been all the
time, amusing himself by finding fresh hiding places
among the bean-stalks by the fence. We all burst out
laughing, which set him at ease again, and the hermit
wasn't even mentioned.

Several times this year he had done things like that.
His mother used to do much the same. If there was any
dispute or upset, no matter how trifling, she would withdraw into herself, turn pale and clench her fists, then
run away and hide. It was almost as if, after she died,
he was trying to take her place and act as she used to
do.

Nino was like her in another way, too. He had long
periods of intense excitement that sometimes made him
tremble, blazing away behind his eyes. I couldn't explain
it, but I realised she was living again in his gestures and
the very words he used. My grief at losing her was always
with me, always beyond all hope of consolation. In me it
fostered rancour and unacknowledged bitterness, the re-
action that always results from the loss of an overstrong
attachment. I wasn't in the least surprised, when I was

C

putting him to bed that night, to hear him order my
sister-in-law out of his room. He almost chased her away,
then 'Papa,' he begged me, 'turn her out of this house.
Send her away or I'll murder her.' His mother would have
said the same.

To calm him down I had to promise I would take him
to visit the hermit, so we cut short our bathe that day.
As we climbed those steep tracks I remember Nino had
to show me the way. He trotted along ahead of me as if
he knew exactly where to go.

'Have you been up here before?' I asked.

'He told me the way,' he replied.

There was a clump of ferns and brambles extending
some way up the side of the hill. The track was almost
impassable and made us sweat, exposed as we were to the
blazing sunshine. We were both drenched by the time
we reached a bare patch of ground. Nino got there first
and turned to call me.

'This poor devil lives in the middle of a nest of vipers,'
I remarked to Nino as I came up to him.

A little path of flag stones laid roughly in line led us
to the black mouth of the cave, protected by a thorny
hedge. Beside the edge of the cliff overhanging the preci-
pice there was a fence of thicket thorns twined around
canes.

We gave a shout, but there was no sign of life. I moved
closer to the cave to pull Nino back from the edge of the
cliff.

'I told you he'd be out among the bushes with his goat
at this time of day,' he said, running ahead of me to
jump over the thorny hedge at the entrance to the
cave.

'Don't go in. It's someone else's home,' I protested.

'There's water inside,' said Nino, 'and I'm thirsty.'

I was amazed at his high spirits. I'd never known him like that before. With some hesitation I peered into the cavern, but Nino ran inside, keeping clear of the thorns. By the time I went in he was already drinking from a ladle. From the back of the cave came the musty smell of a stable. The floor was dry and sandy. Turning back towards the entrance, all I could see was a curtain of climbing plants, blue against the empty sky.

'Let's go back,' I said. 'We're dripping with sweat.'

Nino wanted to light a candle to show me the roof. 'Don't drink any more of that water,' I advised him. 'You don't know whether it's safe.'

'It's very good,' he said breathlessly.

I managed to move away, noting there was only half a cigar in the pocket of a waistcoat hanging on the wall. To tell you the truth, I felt a certain envy for that lay-about who had thought out such a convenient and magnificent way of enjoying himself, living so high above the petty troubles of the countryside and the world itself. As we went down through the ferns, I watched Nino who, sulky with disappointment, ran on ahead of me, never hesitating as to which path to take. Evidently he had climbed this hillside many times before.

I kept talking to him for his own good, interrupted only when we had to cross rivulets swollen by the rain. I was not reproaching him at all, just asking him what kind of job he wanted to do, now that he was nearly thirteen and no longer a child. We often talked about this when going home after our swim. It always ended in our exchanging impressions about the world and our own way of life. I talked to him of my boyhood days, while he interrupted me to talk of his own plans. That evening he was more taciturn than usual, so much so that I began to worry about him.

The following days seemed endless and scorchingly hot — it was mid-August — so sultry that even among those normally wind-swept hills the land was suffering. I needed to inspect more frequently certain fields that belonged to me and lay half an hour's journey from the village. Nino liked going with me and knew all my neighbours. This was where my wife had been born and brought up. We called it 'going to Mama's' when we went there. Sometimes in the afternoon my sister-in-law came with us, glad that when she did so we could not go to the river. I was well aware that if I wanted to please her I should have cut our bathes short, or even given them up altogether. To avoid being anxious about Nino, that good woman had reached the stage of convincing herself that, even for me, it was dangerous to sunbathe so much.

One morning on a market day Nino went out early, hoping to meet the hermit. At one o'clock he still had not come back and I was trembling with anxiety, thinking of the new church being built. I had never managed to prevent Nino going there. His aunt was muttering to herself in the kitchen. When he did appear, exhausted and drenched with sweat, it was she who questioned him. She knew where he had been. People had seen him going towards the river with the hermit. She took off his shoes and found sand between his toes.

What Nino would not admit was that he had gone swimming with a companion without a bathing costume. But if he had been alone, that was even worse. He might have drowned. In the end he confessed that the hermit had kept an eye on him from the bank.

I punished him, without conviction, for it seemed to me simply a revenge for the anxiety we had suffered. Over and over again he repeated: 'Am I drowned, do you think?' His aunt maintained he was as much a vagabond and sinner as the hermit.

That afternoon I took Nino aside and had a serious talk with him. I told him I understood his trouble. I had been a boy myself, too. There was no question of wearing a bathing costume, but it was essential to avoid being deceitful, or endangering himself with the first man who came along. I would have taken him myself, that very evening.

'It's better in the morning,' Nino said.

I tried to put him on his guard against the hermit, telling him he couldn't be much good, a big strong fellow like him, avoiding other people and doing no work himself, living like an animal, depending on charity. Even the cave where he lived didn't belong to him. I asked if Nino had gone to visit him on other occasions.

Nino did not reply, staring indignantly at the wall. No one enjoyed supper that evening, because Nino told me coldly that he was not hungry. He withdrew, having eaten nothing, and when I went to his room he remained silent, his eyes staring wildly as if he had a fever. I touched his forehead. It seemed to me very hot. I told him not to make himself ill if he wanted to come swimming with me tomorrow.

Next morning Nino had disappeared. His bed was still warm, so he had not gone before dawn. As if to give us a second blow the weather, torrid until the previous evening, had changed during the night. The cold flashes of lightning showed up the squalls of rain. I knew Nino was terrified by thunder.

We hunted for him all through the house. We enquired of neighbours; we ran through the fields to look for him; called on houses where he had sometimes taken refuge when he was frightened; as I searched I was bitterly and unjustly blaming it all on his aunt, who looked at me in consternation. Every clap of thunder gave me a fresh shock. Half-way through the morning the rain fell again in floods. Even the river would be swollen. Perhaps Nino had not found even a roof to shelter him. At the first break I ran for the police.

It was midday when I reached home again, exhausted and soaked through. A huge man, blond and hairy, rushed into the piazza, wearing a faded cloak of military cut. When he reached our threshold he opened his cloak and there was Nino, his head and legs dangling like those of a new-born kid. He managed to stand up, looking ashamed.

'This boy was getting stuck in the mud,' he said in a high-pitched raucous voice. Hairs from his fair beard covered his cloak and it stank as a dog does when it is being bathed. Nino stared at him, completely fascinated, though I saw on his cheeks traces of recent tears.

'If, when the better weather comes, you want to come up and breathe good air,' said the gigantic fellow, seriously, 'I won't say no, but keep in mind that every creature, even an animal, has a home of its own.' With a sweep of his cape he took his leave of me and went away, his big feet looking even larger than ever, being encrusted with mud.

We put Nino to bed, afraid he might be feverish, but towards evening, not having said a word, he fell peacefully asleep. Next day he got up more taciturn than ever and deep in thought, refusing to drink his milk. He

looked at me furtively when my sister-in-law began to
question him, and did not answer her. Choosing the right
moment I told my sister-in-law I intended to climb up
to the hermit's cavern to thank him. Nino followed me
into my room and protested against my suggestion. 'The
hermit does not want anyone at all to visit his cave.'

'But you went there yourself?'

'I went to shelter from the rain.'

'At four o'clock in the morning?'

'Don't go there,' he pleaded again. 'He doesn't want
anybody.'

Then I said: 'You're the one who wanted us to go
there, you little fool. You wanted to get away from the
house, wanted me to take you there. You're not a son of
his. He's shown you he has a head on his shoulders.'

'He's a vagabond, Papa.'

'He's a fine man. What harm have we ever done
him?'

In my heart I was trembling more than he was. He
did not answer me. But if in those days he did not try to
run away again, it was certainly not because he wished
to please me.

August was reaching its end. Our first harvests were
practically ready for reaping and discussions on that subject were shattering the calm of our mornings. Waggon
wheels creaked, there was talk of festivities and dances in
neighbouring villages. One day, when I was resting under
the scaffolding of the church (Nino was away in the hay
fields) I heard my name called in a clear voice, almost
jokingly. Above the windowsill appeared the blond head
of the hermit. I was so amazed I could not move for
a moment.

'I've found a house but not a roof,' he said with a

laugh, mopping his forehead. The faces of the builders peered out from behind him.

'Aren't you living up there now?' I asked.

'In the bushes? No. The rural authorities objected. Only animals can go where they like.'

'But you must know some trade or other.'

The hermit gestured as if to say he knew a hundred. His little beard looked very odd, sprinkled with bits of lime.

'If anything occurs to you,' I told him, 'come and see me.'

He listened to me with his eyes half shut, made a sign to show he understood, then disappeared through the window again.

I told Nino all about it, partly out of loyalty and for my own satisfaction, partly because he would have known anyway. That same evening I said to him : 'That hermit isn't a hermit any more. He's a mason now.' Nino listened to me passively and in the morning he crossed the piazza in that direction.

The hermit had found shelter for himself and his goat in a corner partitioned off from a shed belonging to a cobbler. It was so damp that maidenhair ferns were growing there. That night Nino said with a smile : 'It would be healthier if he didn't go to sleep there but spent the time at the inn, sleeping on straw.' I knew Nino wanted to ask me, but did not dare, if we could offer the hermit hospitality ourselves.

Taking the opportunity I suggested it to him myself, but I couldn't bring the hermit into the house. I got him away from the labourers under the portico. He left his work to come and thank me and I asked him to keep an eye on Nino for me, with all that scaffolding about. My other hope was that Nino, who could now see him

whenever he liked, would realise he was just a workman like the others and would get tired of him.

But Pietro was not just a labourer like the others. Some
time or other he had been in some seaport, and larded his
dialect with exotic words that enthralled Nino. Pietro no
longer smelt like a troglodyte. Instead he smelt of lime,
but I knew that his real smell was due to his good health,
his life in the open air and his animal cunning. Compared
with him I felt even older than I did with my son.

During that period, even the river lost its interest for
Nino. More precisely, the river in my company. If Pietro,
who did not like the water, had gone there with him,
Nino would have felt utter bliss.

In September the masons didn't work too hard. The
harvests and the festivities that followed emptied every
workshop. One man would be away cutting hay, another
stacking corn, another preparing the casks. If Pietro and
Nino missed going out together on one day, they would
go out on the next, to some cowshed or an open field.
Soon the wind would bring us the sound of music, songs
accompanied by a harmonica. Once or twice Nino came
running home alone. At other times he came back late
and in a bad temper. Finally he and Pietro came to ask
my permission to stay out until nightfall. This time even
his aunt raised no objection. She was busy preparing for
the coming festivities on the threshing floor.

The ceremony of stripping off the leaves might last
until daybreak. Nino insisted that I should go with them
so that they could stay till the end. Even Pietro urged me
to go too, because: 'There's nothing worse than having
to wait for someone who arrives late.' That was the night
I saw Pietro dancing. Nino came in for several clouts on the
head because he kept following him.

It was dark on the threshing floor. The music was gay and exciting, so was the babble of happy voices. I felt most upset when I noticed that Nino obeyed his friend without grumbling as he always did to me. Towards the end of the party Nino was fit to drop with tiredness. Pietro put him over his shoulder, and thus we went home. As always happens after festivities or any other distractions, neither of us had much to say. The chill of that September night kept us awake.

'Have you got a wife tucked away somewhere?' I asked him.

'No,' he replied with a laugh. 'Never dance twice with the same woman. Flee from temptation!'

'I'm talking of sons. You would be a good father. Look how they all run after you.'

'If I were their father they wouldn't do that. I'd make them work. They'd learn all the more quickly that the only thing that matters is to be happy. If they discover they can manage that for themselves, so much the better. It's true for your son, too.'

At the foot of the hill Pietro took Nino down from his shoulders, stood him on his feet and made him start walking. Nino scarcely opened his eyes, gave each of us a hand and so he came along, his head drooping.

'Was it to keep yourself happy that you became a hermit?'

'It was the women who called me a hermit. They kept coming up to see me — even married ones — and started crossing themselves, so I understood I'd better do the same myself. A man can get along very well alone.'

'I'm worried about that boy of mine. He's always running into danger.'

'He'll grow up, you know.'

As we walked home that night I felt in my heart that Nino was no longer a child. His singing, his lethargy, his longing for adventures in the moonlight, all combined to make me feel that there was something unreal about it, something sad. I almost felt an affection for Pietro. I seemed a mere baby, compared with him.

As I had expected, Nino spent the next day in the garden, idly turning the pages of a book. He came in for dinner looking relaxed and sleepy. We discussed arrangements for the grape harvest. The fruit was already starting to change colour. I asked Nino if he would like to come swimming with me, but he made a face and said he was too tired. His aunt was in a good mood and Nino disappeared until supper time. I felt tired, too, and in some vague way I felt resigned.

When the doctor told me I could reckon on living another month or so and advised me to settle my outstanding bills, I sent for Nino and told him to give his aunt no trouble and not to stay out late. This wasn't quite what I had meant to say, but so many things were whirling around in my mind that I could not tell him anything more. I was ill with fever. Nino took me literally, with an air of uncertainty, as if he had momentarily interrupted a different life of his own.

I lay ill for more than a month. I don't remember the days because for me they did not exist, as days. I went through a period of delirium and unconsciousness. My sister-in-law nursed me well, the doctor came, Pietro came to enquire how I was. I saw Nino once or twice.

When I was convalescent and began to enjoy getting about again, in my weakness I fostered a tender thought that I had been reborn. Nino came to see me. I reverted

to my old habits as if they were new. It was the end of
October now. Nino, too, was living in an unaccustomed
way. We should both have gone back to town, and Nino
should be at school. We ought to be quick about it, or his
studies would suffer.

Nino was more helpful and affectionate. To me he
seemed to have grown and to be more sure of himself,
but when he came home, taking off his mackintosh —
the grape harvest had been finished some time ago —
he wandered round the house answering when spoken
to and behaving like a man who owes nothing to anyone.

His aunt, looking at him indulgently remarked : 'He
hasn't been naughty for months now.' That struck me as
absurd and almost comic. Even Nino smiled.

My first short walks were to the barn, where I learned
that Pietro had been helping with the grape harvest and
other jobs. Now he wasn't working at all, living on the
money he had earned as a mason. Since we had to leave
for the city very soon I went to look for him and suggested
keeping him on as a labourer in the cowshed and dairy,
no longer in the portico but in the stable. Pietro received
my offer kindly but replied that he was going to sell the
goat and resume his travels. The world is wide. So I
tipped him a hundred lire and felt quite relieved.

Mister Peter

I was six years old when my father died and I had reached the age of twenty before I knew anything about a man's rightful position in his own home. By the time I was eighteen I had already made a habit of going off to the fields whenever I could and was firmly convinced that a day without a jaunt of some sort and a chance to play some mischievous trick was a day wasted. My mother did her best to bring me up sternly, as a man would have done. It was entirely due to her that in our home we never exchanged a kiss or spoke an unnecessary word and I had no idea what a normal happy family life could be. Since I was rather delicate and dependent upon her, the emotion she inspired in me was fear, a fear that lay at the root of my attempts to run away from home and my invariable return. When I reached manhood I treated her with a blend of impatience and tolerance, as one would a grandmother.

However, at the time I'm speaking of now I had a job. Even that I owed to her, for she not only made me study hard, she also compelled me to face the challenge of a competitive examination. She took it upon herself to explain to me that, at my age, I ought to be able to support myself. We continued to live in the same house, of course, a place on the outskirts of the town. I liked it because at the front it overlooked the avenue and the

town, and at the back, from the wide windows on the
stairs, it gave a view of fields with clumps of trees in the
distance. Until a year or so ago we had lived in the
country and for me, a green skyline, little paths through
meadows, houses tucked away between woods and reed-
beds, stood for freedom and holidays.

By this time I was spending all day working at a desk
and would come home in the evening to glance through
the staircase windows at the great vault of the sky and
the meadows below, as if to reassure myself they were
still there. When I left work I still had several hours
of daylight ahead of me to spend in walking about, though
I never wandered far from my own neighbourhood. I
often chose to visit the Central Railway Station, to enjoy
the never-ending bustle of the constant comings and
goings, or I would explore the industrial areas where there
were factories, a constant roar of traffic and unexpected
pools of silence and solitude.

One day I went home earlier than usual and heard
voices in our drawing room. Mother called to me brightly
from inside the room, 'Come along in. Come and see who's
here.' I was in one of my awkward moods and paused
by the door, straining my ears to catch any conversation
going on inside, but I soon realised that mother and
her visitor were waiting in silence for me to appear. This
annoyed me so much that I wished I hadn't come upstairs at all, so I went down again, called out something
or other from the landing and went out for another
stroll.

I soon got over my irritation and began making my
way home again, step by step through the dusk. Without in the least wanting to do so I found myself visualis-
ing what would happen when I got there. Mother would

be sitting by the table, looking very cross. In those days
we normally took our meals in the kitchen. Supper for
two is soon over, but I would remain seated until she
started clearing the table. Then I would take refuge in
my own room and sit smoking by the window until dusk
had given way to dark. Often enough I would go out
again, but hardly ventured to do so if it would mean
leaving her alone. On the other side of the wall I would
listen to the movement of her hands as she washed up,
clattering the plates together.

Instead, I found the house ablaze with lights and in
our drawing room a table laid as if for a banquet. Mother
and Mr Peter were there, talking about me. The last
time he had come to see us was fifteen years ago and at
first I didn't recognise him, but he quickly asked me about
a girl called Ninina. Apparently I had been in love with
her in those far-off days. A glance at my mother's eyebrows told me she was annoyed, but she was managing to
smile. By the time we took our seats at table they had
already brought to mind so many escapades of my childhood that it seemed to me we were still living in our
country villa. I recalled those summer evenings when he
and my papa came home together laughing and talking in
the lane leading to our garden gate. I would be waiting
and would run to meet them and fumble in my father's
pockets, until mother appeared at the balcony rail above
the garden. After exchanging greetings they went on
talking across the space between them. I remember pulling his arm, hoping he wouldn't go off home but would
stay and have a meal with us.

Between one course and the next, Mama would rise
from her chair and go to the kitchen, though once he
delayed her by going on talking. I had no idea how to

entertain him, but I rather liked his air of adventure.
He talked to us about his wife, a woman from the Argen-
tine who would be rejoining him in Genoa, where they
were planning to settle. Mr Peter was such a close friend
of my father that between ourselves we used to say that
if he induced father to travel round the world it would be
the death of him. But Mr Peter told us he was an old
man now and wanted to settle down. I noticed that his
quick dark eyes were full of energy, his movements as
vigorous as they had ever been. Far from being old,
Mr Peter seemed to me to be one of those men who have
such a firm, well-balanced grip on life that the passing
years do not change them.

After that first evening he often came to see us. He said
we must be patient with him, for he was a lonely man
and we were the only family he had. He spent his mornings organising various activities that I took to be the
source of his financial security. He wrote long business
letters and waited for telephone calls at his hotel. I
often went there about midday to greet him and to invite
him to come home with me to share our meal. If I had to
wait for him I would sit in his big armchair, watching
people coming and going all around me, and I quite
understood that a man who lived in hotels, felt at home
in railway stations and travelled so widely must obviously
possess a face like his and the same kind of energy. In his
life so far he had seen everything there was to see, had
Mr Peter, and in these early days of our acquaintance
he would talk freely to Mama and me about it, gesturing
with his hands as if to say those times were over now. But
it seemed to me that his voice, the way he talked, the
practised ease he showed in avoiding giving direct answers
to people who questioned him, even the tone he used

when talking to me, might well be due to his way of life in recent years.

Until then I had avoided letting him know I was working for the Town Council, but one day when he and I were walking to my home together, talking of my father, I felt I could do no less than confide in him what kind of job I had. He listened absentmindedly to what I told him, replied vaguely, 'Always do your best,' and returned to some subject that interested him. In our family it had always been a settled thing that my father, if only he had lived, had intended to make a sailor out of me, an officer, so that I should travel and see the world. In my heart I felt grateful to him for planning such a fine life for me. Though Fate had decided otherwise, that didn't stop me dreaming, morning and evening, whenever I was alone, of the day when I would leave home, and start my own world-wide travels. Meanwhile I had to satisfy my urge by walking and walking, going as far as the other side of town, and into the uncultivated waste land of the suburbs. Something might have happened. When I had turned the corner of the last house, under a cool clear sky or the red glow of sunset, the sea might appear before me, an ocean I had never yet seen, vast and teeming with ports, beaches and noise. My idea, or, rather, my conception of this imaginary spectacle, was bound up with my fading memories of my father. I was always very eager to hear anything about him, especially anecdotes revealing his personal characteristics. For instance, I was never tired of listening to Mama telling me of the time he ran away from school when he was fifteen and slept for two nights under a bridge with snow all around. I know now that I was searching among my memories, my instincts, my whole range of conscious knowledge, seeking to trace back to its roots whatever identity my nature had with his, simply because I sensed in him a prediction of my own destiny.

Ever since Mr Peter's first visit, Mama kept praising to him the devotion she said I felt for my father. It bored me stiff. All the same I didn't know how to get myself out of it, and talking with Mr Peter brought it all back again. 'Your father,' he told me, 'was a man who saw things straight. He would even have given the Town Council a kick in the pants, but he knew he would die soon. That knowledge robbed him of any initiative. His illness was taking its course and he persuaded me to say nothing.' It was no news to me that during the years when I was emerging from babyhood, my father was already aware of his approaching death. I could remember an evening, long ago, when he had a kind of fit and his face turned red. He came to the window, shouting hoarsely that he felt suffocated and there was not enough air for him to breathe.

One day Mister Peter asked me, with a furtive glance, 'Are you in love?' I was so furious that I was on the point of leaving him stranded and rushing off home. We were already close to the house though, and if I had run he would have reached it before I could and would have met me by the door, making even more of his sarcastic jokes at my expense. That evening, however, all I did was to re-introduce the subject of the times they had spent together. Mama had always taught me never to give way to anger, reminding me of the example my father had set. Though he knew he was soon to die he went on living, putting up with it all. That evening she remarked that if only Enrico had led the same life as Peter he might not have died. What really killed him was his resignation, his acceptance of imminent death. He had obstinately persisted in keeping his sedentary job and never taking a break. As she came to the end of what she had to say I was surprised at the difference in her voice, more forceful than usual, indeed almost malicious, as if she was harbouring a grudge. It was just as well that Mister Peter started telling us about my father's courting days. He, Mr Peter, had to take charge of the dog while Papa boldly climbed a ladder to deposit a little love letter in a certain pigeon loft. They also met one another at dance halls. At that time Mama had a smart sky-blue dress and when she wore it, it had a certain meaning. If instead she appeared in white it meant the exact opposite. Mama no longer remembered anything about it, nor could they ever find out though they tried hard. 'Enrico would know, perhaps,' Mr Peter remarked, 'if he were still with us.'

One thing I would never have dared to tell anyone, least of all Mr Peter, was that I envied him, particularly because he lived in an hotel and could go in or come out as he chose with no fuss at all. In those few minutes he sometimes kept me waiting I eagerly studied the people and their baggage, their luggage more than the people. Looking at them one by one, their faces were much the same as those of the ordinary men one meets in a street or on a tram, but their suitcases, multicoloured and stuck all over with labels, spoke to me as if they were alive. I never saw a single piece of luggage belonging to Mr Peter, for I always met him in the hotel vestibule, nor did he like talking about his travels, never telling me more than the absolute minimum. He was rather preoccupied with his telephone calls, and when the porter gave him a letter that bore an exotic postage stamp (as I saw at a glance), he barely looked at it and stuffed it into his pocket. Two days later, quite unexpectedly, he told me at the hotel door that his wife had reached Genoa. By tomorrow he would be gone.

He came to a farewell supper at our house, bringing with him some sparkling wine. He needed it to keep up his spirits, he told us. His wife could not tolerate any form of gaiety, and this would be his last drink. Mama watched him absentmindedly but when Mr Peter proposed a toast to the future she raised her eyes, lifted her glass in her bony fingers and with it touched his glass, then mine, very solemnly. I did not look into her eyes because I had already enjoyed a drink or two and was floating along with other drifts of thought. Nor did I look in her face when she told me to go and keep Mr Peter company on his way back to the hotel. I remember she advised both of us to keep warm and not catch cold.

It was a foggy night, and I don't know why I was willing to go out with our guest. Probably it was due to habit, for I had always done so on other occasions, but even to me it seemed impossible for him to leave us like that, as from a social call, without turning to the subject of my father and my own future. Inside himself he was certainly thinking I ought to change my way of life.

The streets were lined with mounds of snow. Between one bank of fog and the next, stars were shining. I remarked to Mr Peter that tomorrow would be a fine day, after a rosy dawn of cloud and sunshine. He ignored the cold and asked me what time I went to the office. I replied that I left home early because, before shutting myself up in my underground cell, I liked to wander through the deserted streets. I worked on the ground floor, in point of fact, but I called it 'underground' almost with tears in my eyes. 'It's really cold,' Mr Peter muttered. 'Shall we have a drink?'

We entered the first place that had a lighted sign showing it was a café. I was on my way to a seat, but Mr Peter ordered two glasses of mulled wine at the bar. 'A man doesn't have to sit down to get warmed up,' he said. 'At your age I didn't do that sort of thing. If I ever made a round of local drinking places as sailors do, it would be from one café to the next.'

I gulped down the wine. Mr Peter drank his slowly, pushing out his lips above his celluloid collar. All the time he had his glass in his hand, he never spoke a word. He really was old, but his light blond hair and his quick darting eyes made him seem an active, lively man. The anaemic dark-haired woman who served us kept watching him out of the corner of her eyes, as if fascinated.

'Do you like this? Are you feeling better now?' he asked when we had finished. Once we were out in the street again he seemed more cheerful and snuggled his neck and chin down into his fur collar, yet his voice sounded despondent as he remarked : 'How many people in the world will do almost anything to keep their heads above water. On the other hand, a glass of wine is all it takes to. . . .' As we came to the entrance of his hotel he was still talking about wine, telling me how difficult it was for a man who was not a landowner to stock a good cellar for himself. He went on to touch upon his ambition to buy a villa, a project he had so far discussed only with my mother. He explained to me that, but for his wife, he would already have settled down in the country. Now he was hoping, at the very least, to get hold of a little house with a vineyard attached. He could send his products overseas from Genoa, where he was well-known. By

now we were inside his hotel, and he said to me : 'Shall
we sample the wine they have here?'

We sat down at a little table in the restaurant attached
to the hotel and he ordered a bottle of vintage wine
that was brought to him by a waiter whom he addressed
as Giacomo. In the light of the table lamp the rich
mellow colour of the wine stood out in sharp contrast
with the white tablecloth. Mr Peter's eyes looked moist
and tender too. Only when the wine was beside him did
he stop chattering.

Why he talked so much, that evening, I had no idea.
My usual awkward shyness melted with that cordial
warmth and the unexpected kindness of Mr Peter. If
my own eyes were watering, it was certainly not due to
grief at our parting. I asked him point blank whether he
couldn't find me a job at sea, perhaps as a steward on one
of his ships. I told him that he must set me free from the
life I was living then, otherwise I should end up as my
own father had done. I was speaking with some heat, and
I remember I didn't dare to stop, for fear of the inevitable
reply.

But Mr Peter looked at me seriously and poured another
glass of wine. He seemed somewhat distressed and his
mouth looked twisted as he muttered that I was a fool.
Why hadn't I told him about it earlier? He didn't own
any ships. 'But I know someone who is in command. It
wouldn't suit you to sign on as a cabin boy. Anyone who
starts at such a low level as that can never rise very far.'
He gave me a sidelong glance and seemed satisfied. 'It
might be your father talking,' he muttered. 'What are you
afraid of? You would be paid from the start, and would
travel first class.'

I told him all I wanted was to get away from the land,

to breathe a different air. I spoke of my father's dream
for me, and my own dreams, too. He fixed his eyes on
me. His own face stood out in the circle of light from the
lamp. His smile was partly mechanical, partly incredu-
lous.

From time to time he questioned me seriously. I talked
to him about sailing ships and embarkation ports. He,
quite warmed up now, spoke of the harbours he knew,
his arrivals and departures, the money he made. We
debated whether sailing boats were better than motor
cruisers. He explained to me (though I knew it already),
that sailing boats are now called 'white flies', out-of-
date relics, fit only for a museum or a nautical school.

When he realised that so far I had never even seen the
sea, the look on his face instantly changed to consternation. He gave my shoulder a friendly squeeze and said :
'Couldn't you come away with me tomorrow?' We talked
over his suggestion and in the end it was agreed between
us that he would write to me from Genoa as soon as he
heard of a good job for me. Soon I noticed how very tired
he looked, utterly exhausted in fact, so I stood up to wish
him goodbye. He didn't move from his seat, but mumbled
something and stretched out his hand to shake mine.

That night I didn't go home at all. Instead I sat in the
station café alone, enjoying my prospects for the future
and relishing my new-found independence. I felt intoxi-
cated, but not with wine. My thought dwelt happily upon
my new clarity of mind. Never have I felt more conscious
of my own courage. Towards dawn I felt very tired but
I couldn't sleep, so I went home, feeling on top of the
world.

It was by no means easy to relieve my mother's
anxieties, but the thought crossed my mind that, before

long, she would have to accustom herself to my being
away from home for a very different reason, though I would
still be a good son to her. Naturally she wouldn't believe
I had spent the night alone, and this idea of her's amused
me very much. Women would be coming along later, but
not yet awhile.

The Sea

Sometimes I think that if I'd only had the guts to climb to the top of the hill that day, I shouldn't have run away from home. It must have been about St John's Night, for already we had several times started out from the valley and had climbed as far as the hazel wood, trying to find the place where the beacon fire stood. We knew that at the very top there were open spaces as large as a meadow. One day Gosto had boasted that when his grandfather was a boy he had followed the road from the valley and climbed so high that he had seen the sea.

The valley road took us through a vineyard that was almost flat and protected by a barrier of hornbeam. What on earth we found to do there all day until evening I simply don't know. We used to watch the tree tops. I told Gosto that nobody would light a bonfire out at sea, because the sea was flat. I stretched myself out on the grass, watching the clouds until I was tired of them. There were crickets in that vineyard and I thought how nice it would be to live like one of them. I could stay there all night and wake up as soon as it was light, before the sun grew warm. We boys were used to seeing the sun always rising behind the low hills from which Gosto's grandfather, as a boy, had seen the sea.

'The sea must be out there somewhere,' I said to Gosto. 'On stormy days that's where it looks wider. Sometimes the sun seems to be shining down on a field of flowers, though with us it's raining hard.' I myself have always imagined the sea must be like a clear sky seen through water. The highway that leads to the hills is not a country road. It runs out from the valley across an open space that slopes sharply, and is flanked by trees, the kinds usually grown in gardens. At a turn in the road, after it leaves the valley and crosses the iron bridge, stands a pretty little house with a balcony full of geraniums, the home of the Piana family. At this level there are no vineyards, no farm buildings, no clumps of trees. Farm carts drawn by oxen never come up from the valley, but on the main road there is a constant stream of carriages with ladies carrying parasols.

All through St John's Night, Gosto had been running about wherever he liked. I couldn't go with him because in our house we all sit out on the terrace to watch the bonfires. Gosto waited for me on the road by our garden gate, and with cries of excitement we pointed out to each other the biggest beacon fires or those that were farthest away. Then the music-makers came by, visiting every part of the village as they always do on St John's Night. Everybody was there, even Candido. I rattled the bars of the gate and called out to him. Candido paused to greet my sisters and exchange a laughing remark, then still playing, he fell back into line. By now, Gosto had joined them and they all marched away to the market place. All night long I could hear Candido's clarinet. There were trombones and guitars as well. All the villagers were singing at the top of their voices, especially the women. When the last bonfires had gone out and the hills were dark again, we all went to bed. I was crying with rage, but as I lay listening to drunken voices and the barking of dogs in the distance, my thoughts turned to my vineyard in the valley, the carriages on the road and the hills I'd be happy to see again tomorrow. Next day, however, we still went no higher than the clump of trees.

Gosto's grandmother was always urging him to model his behaviour on mine. It made Gosto laugh. In my home my relatives were forever telling me to copy him. Gosto and his grandmother were the only members of his family left in the whole world and he seldom forgot his position as head of the house. There's no point now in telling anyone about the things we did at school in Alba. They wouldn't believe me. They just keep on and on, telling me Gosto is more of a man than I am. No one knows the arguments that go on in my home.

However, this idea about the sea came to me, not to him. Gosto doesn't know what it's like to stand looking at a house until it no longer seems a house at all. Gosto himself is so free that he does whatever he is told, but if he is left alone he does nothing. Even now he won't believe me when I explain to him that the main roads never come to an end, nor do the railway lines. They run from one place to another without a break as long as there is land. He says that if this were so, people would never stop walking. Everyone would want to go all round the world, and our main road would be thronged, this way and that, with foreigners from other countries.

'All roads end at the sea,' I told him. 'That's where the ports are. You could get on a boat and go out among the islands, where roads begin again.' He was by no means convinced that, to get to the sea, all you have to do is to start walking. 'You'd need to know the road,' he said.

'The road knows where it leads to,' I told him. 'From

here you'd go past the little house with the geraniums.'

'Will it be far away?' he asked.

'If your grandfather saw it from the Ca' Rosse. . . .
How many years ago was that?'

One day we went to the wheelwright's workshop. We
had to take a roundabout road because we weren't used
to going barefoot. I stood by the entrance and could see
almost nothing inside, where it was dark, except for the
glow of the blacksmith's fire, but I could hear Pietro
hammering on iron. Pietro asked me if I went to school
with Gosto, and told us that when he was our age he had
already travelled beyond the mountains, looking for work.
What skills had we learned that would get us a job?
That's when I realised we knew nothing. At that moment
Pietro stopped hammering and I heard Gosto say 'Fellows
like us are born with shoes on.'

'So that's how it is,' Pietro replied, not in the least
offended. 'You were born with shoes on.'

I thought a good deal about what Pietro had said, and
next day we went back to his workshop to continue the
conversation. Pietro was still working at his fire and called
to us to get out of his light. That day he told us that as
a boy he had learned to be a locksmith. He and his master
had travelled about, looking for work in blacksmiths'
yards, carrying behind them their tools and some coal.
To go over the mountains they'd had to wear rope-
soled shoes. Then they'd worked as coalminers in a place
so far away that to return home they'd had to take a
train. As he talked to us he came to the door and looked
out across the piazza.

'But the sea, Pietro! Didn't you see the sea?' Gosto
asked him. Then he told us that he had been to Marseilles,
where the sea was just outside his door. He gazed across

the piazza, where his house was casting a shadow, and
said : 'What was it like? Like this piazza, where there's
always something going on, day and night, worse than in
a big market.' He spat towards the sun and went back
inside.

We asked him what the sea-shore was like, but either he
didn't know or didn't understand our question. Then he
said : 'The water is green and always in motion, con-
tinually throwing up scum. I've never been on the water,
and I don't know what the land looks like from the open
sea. I'm told the colour of buildings is something between
red and black and the port smells like a railway station.
In a port, more coal is loaded and unloaded in a day
than the weight of all the grapes on our hills. The sailors,
even when they are foreigners, dress the same as we do.
All they think of is when can they go back home again.
The coast frets the sea. You'd need to be born with shoes
on if you want to live there.'

It was the month of August, between the first and
second harvest, when nothing is done in our village except
getting in the grapes and the day's work takes half the
night as well. I was sent to bed when it was dark outside.
From the road below the terrace I could hear people
laughing and walking about. If I had done anything
naughty I was sent to bed. If Gosto came to call for me,
they would tell him it was late and I'd been asleep for
some time.

Every now and then my family would go over to Belbo.
To me it was even more boring than staying at home,
where I could at least read the papers and magazines. I
had a cupboard full of them. Late one afternoon I was
reading on the terrace when I heard Gosto calling to me
from the road. I shouted back at him. He told me to

listen. Something was going on down there. Then I heard voices a long way off, just as one does in September when working between the vines. I noticed that the music carried to me by the wind earlier in the afternoon had stopped now. There had been wedding festivities at Martino yesterday and people had seen guests being taken home in hired carriages early this morning. Candido, the trombonists and a group of musicians called the Octovini had been playing continuously ever since the previous evening.

'There's another fire,' Gosto yelled, and my sisters came out on the terrace to watch. The sun was so bright that we could hardly see, but the air above the trees seemed to be quivering. Someone shouted they could hear women weeping. From all the houses around everybody ran out into the road, all talking at once and scrambling over piles of rubble. Old women were calling for help. Gosto told me that a young man, a farm labourer, dripping with sweat, had run past him, making for open country. At last we could all see the smoke rising from the far side of the hill, shimmering as if it were under water.

My family called to me not to go away, but I was already down in the road with Gosto, so they couldn't stop me. I replied that everyone was going. Candido was up there. The papers and magazines could stay on the terrace. Gosto came running, eager to show me the way.

I had never seen him so red and so excited as he looked then. We could now see a column of smoke rising beyond a field of maize and hear the crackling of the flames. Everyone started to bellow like a bull, shouting 'The fire! Fire!' But then we fell silent, out of respect for our masters. One of them pushed his way into that farmyard,

yelling and kicking at piles of rubbish. If he had not been
held back he would have gone into the house too.

The yard was full of bits and pieces thrown out of the
windows and doors. In the middle of it there were dozens
of rabbits. Several women were carrying away items from
the rubbish heap. One of them, struggling to take a huge
mattress, got stuck in the door. No one said a word. All
we could hear was the roar of flames from the sheds,
and every now and then a voice giving orders.

Luckily the wind was carrying the smoke and sparks
towards the vineyard. The heat was scorching, and the
three or four men who had been drawing buckets of
water from the well, ready to give them to the boys
running around everywhere, changed their minds and
plunged their faces into the water, thoroughly drenching
themselves. Gosto had been strolling around between the
tables, still loaded with remnants of the wedding feast,
and he gave me a sign to come and help myself. I knew
almost everybody in the yard and recognised the bride,
dressed in red, sitting on a kitchen chair in hot sunshine
wearing her fine shoes and stockings. She was gazing
across the yard with an air of dignity and pride as if all
this was no business of hers. I gathered she had been
weeping, and no one ventured to speak to her.

They were talking together under the walnut tree,
calling one another by name. They caught sight of Gosto
and me and we told them who we were. It seemed like a
Sunday when we passed below the terrace, on our way
back to the village. One man was sitting eating, and from
behind the house came several men in their shirtsleeves
bathed in sweat. The bridegroom was cursing. They poured
out some beer for themselves, said something I didn't
hear, then slapped one another on the neck to drive off

the flies. Before nightfall I went up again to see if there were any flames. The inside of the house was completely gutted. The sheds and other buildings were open to the sky and still smoking, giving off a dreadful heat. I saw Candido spreading out black bundles of burnt hay with a pitchfork. He didn't speak but winked without a smile and gestured to me to go away.

Discussions were still going on in the yard. Now, women and men, local farmers and the bride were all together under the walnut tree. One would exclaim, another remain silent, another would kick at a hoe.

Gosto and I went all round the yard, looking at the beds, cupboards, all kinds of household goods broken or torn to shreds. Now for the first time I understood what harsh events these people have to face, their fears and anxieties went far deeper than the fire. They knew what accusations might be made against them, what malicious gossip they might have to endure from neighbours who considered them 'bad blood'.

'I can't get married and look after the cowshed at the same time,' the bridegroom complained, still wearing round his neck the ceremonial silk handkerchief. 'If instead of listening to music you'd kept a better watch,' an old crone said through her teeth. 'But that girl of yours wanted music. . . .' I saw Candido coming over from the back of the house and they all stopped talking. Then they started a discussion on a different subject : what was to be done with the straw they had left.

From the kitchen railing one could look into the empty rooms, their walls broken open. The walls showed marks where furniture had stood, festoons of paper decorations still hung there. Outside, boys were chasing rabbits, shouting excitedly. A barefooted woman went into the kitchen from the path outside and quickly ran out again, saying the flagstones were still hot.

I knew it was late by now. Gosto had told me that the cattle must be rounded up before nightfall. They had got away from the damaged cowsheds. Under the shade of the trees everyone was discussing the best way to do the job. They decided to form separate teams, leaving the women out of it. That night the bride would sleep at the Piana family's home, but before starting out over the stony tracks of Belbo a meal was essential. A table was laid for twenty people or more. Meanwhile Candido and his team had rounded up the cattle from the open country. We boys were forbidden to move. A bull had been burned and would soon do his best to gore us if we did. The cool air brought to us the sound of voices. Candido and his team were now working up in the vineyard.

While Gosto was rummaging round the courtyard, I strolled about under the walnut trees and listened to the women who had to get to the Piana's house. The road to the hills continued from outside the house. Beyond those hills lies the sea. Getting there is only a question of time. As I stood looking out between the trunks of the walnut trees, the whole valley lay open before my eyes, sloping downwards. Once beyond the plain of Belbo, a man would be in a different country.

I was strolling in the shade of the trees when one of the women, Clelia Piana, called me over and asked me if I wasn't going to have supper with the bride. I noticed that Gosto was already sitting at table and eating heartily. I was given meat, salame and pancakes, but I didn't eat much. I drank wine and called across the table to Gosto, 'Here's good health!'

The bride, Clelia, and some other girls started talking

D'

to Gosto and me. They enquired after my sisters and
asked why they hadn't come to the wedding. An old
woman said that we who lived near the village were too
proud. 'We've come to represent them,' Gosto said with
his mouth very full. 'Do they know you're here?' Clelia
asked me with a smile.

When we set out for the Piana's house it was already
dusk. Two or three of Candido's group of musicians
came with us for company. Gosto and I walked in the
middle of them and the women. By the time we were
half-way there it was dark. When we came to the main
road someone started playing the guitar and the girls
began to sing, two of them walking arm in arm with the
bride. Some fellows and the girls had stayed behind and
we heard them laughing and calling to one another as
they followed the track marked by white stones, beyond
the meadows. I walked beside Gosto and said to him :
'What a lovely night we've had!' 'You could say that,' he
replied.

Not all of us were singing. Some girls were walking
two by two, talking to each other. There was one fellow
who kept running from one group to another as dogs
do. I myself stayed near to Clelia because I liked hearing
her sing.

When we got to the farmhouse the bride started weeping again because her husband, instead of coming to sleep
with her, had to work all night. Everybody, young and
old, told her to be patient. Her husband had been
rounding up the cattle and would soon be back again.
Clelia and a few others crossed the yard with her and
went inside. Then the musicians, the Octovini and a
guitarist, started the traditional serenade, by the light of
a lamp brought from the hayloft.

The rest of us stayed on the road, in complete darkness. The house where the geraniums were growing was by the next turn in the road, a hundred yards farther on. I said to Gosto: 'If they see us now they'll send us home.' 'You're crazy,' he replied. 'Let's go on.'

After all we had done together that day it almost came as a surprise that we'd have to separate. Gosto grumbled that it had taken the idea of having supper with the bride to make up his mind. 'There will be other fires, other wedding festivities,' he told me. I was well aware that by now my family would be thinking I'd run away from home.

The night was so dark that all we could see was the stars. We took a step or two as if we had never walked along this road before. Gosto was still light-headed from the wine he had drunk, and was talking about the fire, laughing and dancing in the road. 'People like us,' he said, 'should go to weddings all the time.'

While he was talking he couldn't keep pace with me, and kept calling me to wait for him. 'If the Martini's place had burned down at night,' he said, 'what a fine bonfire it would have made!' As we came to the stretch of road where the trees seemed to be closing in on us, even Gosto managed to step out more briskly. Not that we felt frightened, but it seemed best to keep talking and laughing. When we came to the house with the geraniums, Gosto started singing and calling out as if someone he knew was living there. Far away behind us we could still hear singing. I told Gosto to shut up. The last thing we heard from inside the house was a woman's voice, saying: 'See to the fire, Clelia.' I stared out into the darkness, hardly daring to breathe. By now we had reached the main road and the very air had a perfume of its own. Gosto ran ahead of me then.

The road made a sharp turn, following the rim of the valley. There were now no trees overhanging the road to scare us. There was a steep bank beside the road, and from it we found ourselves looking out into nothingness. Far below us lay the flat plain of Belbo, now lit only by the stars. The factories on the far side of the valley, that all day long were ablaze with yellow lights, now showed not a glimmer. Looking down at them was like looking down a well. Everywhere was black and the wind seemed to shake the stars.

'What a lot of fires we've seen tonight!' Gosto remarked. 'Do you want to see another?'

'Silly ass!' I retorted. 'That's Cassinasco's factory. Let's stop and listen. Somebody may be shouting.' But all we could hear was the sound of the crickets so we went back to the road. Gosto kept telling me there was a fire down below us, so we ran back up the hill a little way to get a wider view. 'I want to see a fire at night,' he said, running up to the next turn in the road. The valley looked farther away now, and we could see in the distance several hills, black against the sky. 'Don't make a noise,' I told him. 'Someone may hear us.' We strained our ears to discover whether the serenade was over, and this time we were alone with the crickets. Gosto had sobered up and now realised that shouting simply increased one's fear.

He threw himself down on the grass and wanted to stay there. I told him we ought to get home, or at least as far as Robini's place, where we might find a haystack or a pile of straw. Just then we heard a cock crowing, heaven knows where. 'Look here,' I said. 'It's nearly dawn and we're still where we were.' (Gosto didn't know that cocks sometimes crow all night long.) We started walking

on down, looking all round us to see if the first light of
dawn was in the sky. We wanted to reach the hills ahead
of us before dawn. We passed Robini's place and several
other buildings. Under the stars we could hardly see the
dark countryside, but we could smell it.

Who could say how long that night had lasted! We
had no need to turn back. Soon we were down on level
ground, walking between gardens and villas. First of all
we heard cocks crowing up on the hills. By now Gosto was
staggering, and no longer replied to anything I said. Every
time there were trees hanging over our path I looked at
him and felt I was alone. I knew that only the moon
could help us now. Had it already risen and set? It was
so late. Even the crickets were quiet by this time. I knew
that a wind would blow up before daybreak, but everything around us, bushes, trees, the very road itself was
silent.

The worst thing about it was that walking in the dark,
with Gosto on his feet but asleep, I started thinking of
home and the festivities of bonfire night, when everybody
else was out in the street and I had been sent to bed.
Gosto was right, I decided. Bonfires and weddings were
essential for people who wanted to escape from mono-
tonous routine, as we had done. Walking along in the
darkness I was thinking hard, imagining that every bend
in the road would bring us to the sea-shore. Then we
would stop walking and creep under a bridge to sleep
under cover. It seemed to me that the sea must exist
only at night. I didn't tell Gosto anything about this. It
was no good discussing such things with him. When we
woke up under the bridge in sunshine I noticed that
beyond the archway a little stream of water was flowing
between the plants, so I decided that Belbo itself was

by the sea and the sand we had slept on must be a beach.

Under that bridge we met Rocco. Gosto woke up before I did and found him bathing his eyes. Later on I tried to find out whether he had been near us in the darkness and might have heard anything I'd said to Gosto as we were dropping off to sleep, but I couldn't get him to say. We spent some time looking around the place and the only thing Rocco asked us was whether we had come far from home. Gosto told him our house had been burned down. Later on he told me that Rocco had never seen us or known anything about us. What did it matter, anyway? If we wanted to get away, all we had to do was come out from under the bridge and go somewhere else. But Rocco followed us. He climbed much faster than we could.

Just beyond the bridge was an avenue of plane trees. Along this avenue, facing the sun, came a carriage drawn by a trotting horse that held its head to one side as if it was feeling skittish. Only a couple of paces farther on stood the hill, a pretty hill the colour of white grapes and quite low. I stopped and suggested to Gosto we should let that Rocco fellow go on ahead. There was something I wanted to remember. For a little while I hid behind the foliage of the plane trees, watching him, listening without turning round. The horse had stopped trotting. The conviction came over me that I had seen all this before — the low hill, the bright sunshine. I remembered the echo, too. This was not my first visit.

A couple of yards further on, hiding behind the trees, Gosto was waiting for me. Some way ahead I saw old Rocco in rags and tatters, with the strong stick he used for walking. Not once did he look back. 'He's gone now,'

Gosto told me. Beyond the plane trees we came to the first of the villas of Canelli and kept a good lookout as we passed them. I don't know why, but we kept walking in the middle of the road, not on the pavement. Consequently all the people knew we were strangers arriving from somewhere outside. Gosto was talking all the time. He didn't even know that at this time of day it's wise to keep a good lookout. I liked the balconies and the roof gardens overlooking the alleyways, for I had never before in my life seen flowers like those in Canelli. I looked everywhere, especially at the people strolling up and down the streets. In the market place we found a fountain like the one in Alba and ran over to quench our thirst. Gosto came second and gave me a kick or two but I kept on drinking, telling him he couldn't really be thirsty after all the wine he had drunk with the bride. 'That's what's made me thirsty,' he said. At that moment I heard Rocco's voice again.

He had opened his bundle on the wooden seat and was untying one of his shoes. The sole of it was worn through and he was changing the position of a piece of protective material placed inside. He was talking to himself, saying it was wrong to waste water.

'So much of it runs away,' Gosto replied, 'and the market place belongs to everybody.' Rocco did not answer him and finished tying on his shoe. Then he stood up, washed his fingers in the fountain and wiped them on a filthy rag, reminding me of what ladies do after eating peaches. Rocco sat down again, opened his bundle and took out some bread and cheese. 'Go back home,' he muttered, 'Go home.'

'Let's go on,' I said to Gosto. 'We'll get a meal at the Cassinasco place.' 'How did he know we were running away?' exclaimed Gosto when we reached the other side of the square. I replied, 'That's your fault. You kept chattering to him under the bridge, all about the fire and the bride.' 'Would you believe it? An old tramp like him understanding!'

'We ought to go back by September,' Gosto went on. 'When the grapes have all been gathered, what can we find to eat?'

'Let's get to the Cassinasco place. Then we'll see.'

But instead we turned our heads to see what Rocco was doing. This time we stayed on the pavement. The sun was blazing down on the market square and Rocco couldn't stay there long. We watched him finish eating his bread. When he stood up, a gang of Canelli boys arrived at the fountain and started throwing water at one another. Rocco quietened them, took another drink, and then crossed to the other side of the square and turned the corner.

We followed him as quickly as we could. Gosto, quite happy again, began larking about as he had done earlier, on the road. I enjoyed it too, all the more because Rocco came out from a field and started walking in the same direction as ourselves. The low hill now seemed close enough for us to touch it. Rocco did not turn, and as we drew level with him Gosto said, 'So long, dad!'

Rocco showed no surprise. When Gosto remarked to him that it was cooler to walk at night, he replied he didn't think that was a good idea because you couldn't see where to put your feet and would damage your shoes. We went along the base of the hill that had been in front of us at first. Rocco turned aside along a little alley where there were piles of rubbish. Gosto followed him and I stayed where I was.

'Come along with Rocco,' Gosto said.

'You don't even know where we're going.' I replied.

So as not to waste the morning we stayed where we were. There were little hills like this one back home too. Gosto was jumping round Rocco, telling him what a huge fire ours had been. Our cattle had all died in their stalls. He said our family had told us to clear out. They couldn't be bothered with us because they were too busy assessing the claim for damages.

'It looks as if we'll have to go to San Libera,' I said to Gosto.

'Here's the vineyard of the parish priest,' Rocco re-marked, coming to a halt and raising his stick.

There was nothing to be seen except the sky and a large fig tree bearing white fruit, the first tree in the row. Gosto said: 'We're all right this time.' We jumped over the thorny hedge and started picking the fruit. 'Not to eat, though,' I told him. 'We'll eat later on.' While Gosto was climbing the tree I looked round. Rocco was nowhere to be seen. 'Be careful the figs don't give you away,' I cautioned Gosto. To eat them we went farther along the narrow track looking for a suitable place. We were already sitting down on the grass when we caught sight of Rocco's stick and then the man himself, waiting for us. 'They must be dried,' he told us, 'then they can be eaten in the winter.' As if he had bought them he shared out, two by two, a handful of the finest fruit. Gosto had to poke his nose in and say: 'I call it stealing.' He put his pile aside. 'It was you who stole them,' Rocco told him.

The morning was over when we reached the place Rocco called home. It had a stone wall facing the valley behind the hill. There was no yard, there was nothing at all. Obviously Rocco was living on charity. 'Have you any money?' we asked him. 'A man doesn't need money,' he replied. Looking at the house, Gosto went crazy. 'See how lovely it is here!' He asked Rocco whether he lived there in the winter. Rocco invited us to go into a room. It was full of pumpkins, stalks of maize, apples to be dried and heaps of grass. It smelt like a farmyard at harvest time. Rocco, near the window, had picked up his bundle and was taking out the figs. He waved his hand in a typical old man's gesture and said: 'This is mine.'

It was hard to get Gosto away from there. Outside the sun was blazing down. He told me that as long as we hadn't had a midday meal it was still morning. We had plenty of time. 'Can't you see,' he said, 'how grand it would be to stay here? We could go into Canelli whenever we liked. We could fish in the Belbo.' 'Is it worth the trouble of walking all night just to catch fish in the Belbo? I'm not stopping here,' I told him. 'Not stopping?' 'No. I won't stay here.' He said, 'We're only three hours from home. We can come back here whenever we like.'

We were talking by the door so that Rocco couldn't hear us. 'So you won't come along with me?' I asked him dryly. Gosto shrugged his shoulders without speaking, so I said, 'I'm going now.' Just then Rocco broke into our conversation, telling us to go and get some grass for his rabbits. This time I was the one to give a shrug, and Gosto said: 'Aren't you going to give us a slap-up meal?' 'First get the grass,' Rocco insisted, so we went back to the valley to gather grass. Gosto kept running to the top of a meadow and then came rollling down. Over and over I told him I meant to be by the Cassinasco works sometime that evening. 'There's no need to start this very minute,' he argued. 'Why do you want to go up there? You can't see the sea from there.'

I knew there was no glimpse of the sea from that level. I had known it ever since we thought we were at the Ca' Rosse, but I hadn't said anything about it to Gosto. When the sack was full of grass, back we went to Rocco. He gave us some bits of bread and allowed us to smear it with garlic. He put his into water with a little salt, to make soup. 'Sometime today that maize should be threshed.' Gosto changed the subject by talking about the hill by the Cassinasco place and asking what could be seen from the top of it. 'The clock tower of Bubbio,' Rocco said. 'Doesn't the hill end there?' I asked him. 'Then there's Nizza.'

Gosto said : 'You've got about a lot, old fellow. Haven't you ever seen the sea?' 'What sea?' Rocco asked him. We got away that afternoon, Gosto running after me and calling out for me to wait till he caught up. 'Rocco gave us something to eat,' he said. 'so we should have threshed his maize for him.'

By now we had reached the fig tree. 'It's not worth the bother of running from home just to gather grass for rabbits. We'll have to think about that tonight. We can't turn back now.'

'It's a shame about that fire,' he said, and I replied : 'Silly ass. We'll see plenty of others tonight.' We walked through Canelli and stopped by the square.

Gosto really got a move on now, trotting like a horse along the avenues of plane trees. I took the road we had come by, running until I was well away from the place, in case the boys of Canelli had it in for us. This time I took the higher road. Turning to look back to the square, I realised I was now alone, and I was glad of it.

Now it didn't matter in the least to me that I hadn't had a glimpse of the sea from Cassinasco. It was enough

for me to know it was there, beyond the fields and the
hills. I was thinking hard as I walked between hedges.
I thought all the afternoon because the slope of the hill
was so gradual that anyone looking at it thinks he's
reached the top but he never does. At every bend in the
road there were terraces, gardens and balconies, and I
took a great interest in them from the start, especially
when a plant had a leaf or a colour I'd never seen
before. For a whole hour I met nobody and saw nothing
except an occasional farm cart. If a man stood still a
moment, he could smell the vines beyond the hedges and
see the supporting canes. That's a lovely thing about
Canelli. It seems a long way off, in a countryside different
from ours, the hill no longer seems to be a hill, even the
sky seems brighter, as it does when there is sunshine and
rain both together, but the people cultivate their land
and work on their grapes just as we do.

Towards evening I came to the pine-trees of Cassinasco.
Gosto should have reached home by now. I walked the
final stretch of road, thinking about nothing at all. A
hedge of blackberry bushes shut off my view. Before me
and behind me, women and farm labourers were going
along the road to the crest of the hill. I had the sun at
my back and my shadow fell across the blackberry bushes.
The houses in Cassinasco were small and dark, though the
sun blazed down on them as it did on the church. At last
I came out beyond the village. I saw another hill and the
empty sky.

I paused to look around while there was enough light to
see by. As I did so I thought about what Gosto had
said by the house and about the good supper he was
probably enjoying this very minute. Perhaps Gosto was
still somewhere on the road. People at home would think

we must be dead. I stretched out on the grass as I had
done under the walnut trees, refreshing myself by looking
at the sky. I did not feel hungry. It seemed to me as if
I'd already been in bed for some time. I fell asleep.

I really did sleep, and when I woke up it was night. I
had been dreaming of the fire and hearing voices as
if they were calling me. The sky was full of stars and I
thought Gosto might be somewhere near me, among the
trees. But no, I was still alone. The bushes near me were
lit up by a red reflection that filled the road with light.

People were walking along the road, talking and calling to one another, all making their way towards a bonfire in a field beyond the trees. It was an enormous fire,
filling the darkness with light. When people stopped
talking for a moment I could hear it biting into the fuel
and crackling with little explosions, so I also ran to the
field. It was full of boys dancing and rolling about, and
men pushing over wood and bundles of sticks, but they
couldn't go closer than five paces because of the heat. I
kept shouting 'Gosto! Gosto.'

It went on for more than two hours. Other bonfires
were blazing all over the hills, but ours was one of the
largest. The boys of Cassinasco talked to me about it and
punched me in the back because I had confused a bonfire
with the lights of a cheese factory.

We ran to see which of us could manage to pull a
burning piece of wood from the blazing heap. A big lad
who saw me in the light from the fire asked me who I
was. I told him that on St John's Night in our village
we always had a band that played the whole time. 'Don't
worry,' he told me. 'Our festivities take place tomorrow.
We have a band, too.'

Every now and then we heard a voice squealing with

fright. Then men ran over and started to laugh because the girls were waiting for them. A man caught hold of me as I stooped to pick up a branch. 'Are you mad?' he exclaimed. 'What if you fell in the fire?' I struck him with the branch and ran off into the darkness with some other boys. They threw the branch, still burning, out on the road. I heard a woman's voice scream loudly, then came laughter and the sound of a fist fight. 'Perhaps Gosto is there,' I thought. The flames were now high enough to light the whole valley. 'Who knows,' I said to myself, 'whether they can see the sea from the top.' Every time anyone threw on another bundle of wood I looked down into the valley to see if the River Belbo had caught fire. I had a great desire to find an open space between the trees where I could dance about and see everything that was going on down there.

Every now and again someone started singing, but there was no band like Candido's. They were just expending their breath, not singing at all. The fire was dying down into ashes and everybody was talking of going to get a drink. We boys stayed behind to turn everything upside down, especially the metal containers that caused an echo. I made friends with a boy called Maurizio who seemed about my age, but in the darkness I could not see him clearly. He told me he came from the woods in a cart bringing all his family to enjoy the festivities. He had put on new shoes that morning.

Maurizio laughed when I told him that shoes would rub the skin from his feet. He lost them that same night when, with some of the others, he had run down to hear the music from the door of the inn. It was full of people. There were only three musicians, but they played so loudly that I couldn't bear listening to them in an enclosed space. I spent the night between the square and the inn door. Glasses of wine were already poured out on tables, but when I asked for a drink they gave me water. I had agreed with Maurizio to spend the night sleeping on the straw in his cart, but he hadn't waited for me.

At first daylight I spent some time walking around the place where the bonfire had been. Sparrows were twittering now and I could not get to sleep again. The bushes around me turned pink, then red and at last the sun rose behind the hill. One thing I knew for certain. The sun must be shining over the sea as well as the land. The ashes of the fire were white now. I smiled as the thought struck me that at home someone would be lighting the fire at this very moment. But I was hungry: I was hungry and my bones felt ready to break.

All the morning I walked along the roads by the crest of the ridge, bathing my feet in the grass and eating blackberries. Between the trees I saw the top of the other hill, just as, at home, I could see Cassinasco. In this part of the country, as everywhere else, there are some boorish people. The inn door opened and a servant came out, but she would not listen to a word I said. She just threw out a bucket of water.

If I had found Maurizio I could have had something to eat, but how could I find him? I had seen him only by the light of the flames. So I went away from that valley, for country folk are the same everywhere. There were no more bushes with ripe fruit, and the apple trees were too close to the houses. I should be seen from the windows. Everybody seemed to be coming out of doors now, I could hear them talking all round me, so I threw myself down on the grass in a dry ditch by the roadside. If people ever found me they would understand I had died of hunger. 'What can I do?' I said to myself as I nodded off to sleep again.

I woke up when the sun was burning me, and I heard a noise. It came from a cricket on a bush. There was no one on the road now but I could still hear voices. They seemed to come from the hill in front, carried by the wind.

It was then I thought about going back down to Cassinasco, where I had seen bundles of canes being delivered. There might be a fig or two underneath those canes. Anyway I couldn't get home tonight, as I expected Gosto had probably managed to do. I had hardly set foot on the road when I saw Candido walking towards me, his clarinet under his arm.

'What's all this?' he asked as he halted beside me.

'I'm here all right,' I replied. One of the good things about Candido is that he never talks down to me as if I were a child. He listens to what I say and thinks it over. 'Where's Gosto? Have you left him behind?'

'Gosto turned back yesterday. He wanted to go home. Haven't you seen him?'

'We were out searching for you both all day, down by the Belbo,' he told me, the same expression on his face as when he talked to me at the Martini's place. He was not smiling. 'Yesterday we reported that you were missing and had probably fallen down exhausted.'

I shrugged and told him I was already in Cassinasco by that time. Candido looked up and down the road, then at the hill. A cart came along with people in it. They called out to Candido. I couldn't catch what they said, but I heard Candido wish them good evening. 'Evening already?' I asked.

'Come on down,' Candido suggested. 'Let's go and see what we can do.' First of all we looked for the telephone exchange. The operator was a girl very much like my sister. She was a friend of Candido, and they shared a joke or two, waiting for a line to be available. Candido gave the phone number of my home and went on chatting to the girl, saying he would be playing for the dances all night. 'D'you really want to go back home?' he asked. The girl stayed close beside us to listen, and asked him with a smile if he ever managed to have a dance himself. 'You won't find time for one tonight,' I said. 'It's already taken me two days to get here.' 'You know what that road is like,' Candido remarked. I realised he had spoken vaguely so that I should not feel embarrassed in front of the girl.

At last the phone bell rang, and Candido spoke first. 'They're all coming to talk to you,' he told me. He let them know we were at Cassinasco but they didn't understand and when it was my turn to talk I felt too nervous to say a word. They didn't grumble at me. They asked me where I had slept, they were full of exclamations and got in touch with the exchange themselves. They wanted me to come home at once. I felt sick with rage that the girl should know all this, but she was still talking to Candido so I dropped my voice and asked if mamma was all right. 'Mamma is waiting for you, silly boy.' I replied that I would come home with Candido and stay with him all the time. They wanted to talk to him again, but just then another voice broke in to say our time was up, so I shouted, 'We'll be home tomorrow,' and put the receiver down quickly.

We went to have supper at a house close to the edge of the valley. Its courtyard was roofed in with growing

vines, and the other musicians were already there. They
all knew Candido and were waiting for him. The courtyard looked out towards the other hill. In the kitchen
there was a huge fire almost as big as the bonfire. Women
were rushing about in every direction. Candido mentioned
that I'd had nothing to eat since yesterday and the
women, shocked and alarmed, brought me a plate with
bread and some grapes, the kind that ripen in July. They
asked me what I'd been doing, but I couldn't talk with
my mouth full. I had found a seat on the box of fire-
wood, close enough to the fire to feel its heat and savour
the smell of roasting meat. I could hear a loud noise from
the pastry boards where women were kneading dough.
Through the doorway I could see the hill and the bit of
sky. Nothing was better than the thought that now I was
with Candido and had talked to my family. Not one of
them knew that farther down there was the sea. The hill
was shaped like a cloud. If I shut my eyes a little all I
could see was the trunk of the vines.

'Don't eat too much,' Candido advised me. 'There's
roast lamb to follow.'

We went out into the courtyard, where men were talking and drinking. They were standing as they drank, and
again I felt I was still under the walnut trees at the
Martini's place.

'Did you round up all the cattle?' I asked Candido.

'Two of them got away beyond the Belbo,' he replied,
his expression giving nothing away.

Then, while the other players were calling for him, I
told him Gosto was a fool because he wanted to stay with
an old tramp beside the Belbo who had sent us both out
to get grass. He let me finish my story and then said:
'Coming to Cassinasco in festival time is not enough.

What did you think you'd find? This place doesn't lead
anywhere.'

Without giving me a chance to reply he looked at the
others and said to me: 'Make your mind up. Sometime
I'll do the same as you.' Now everybody in the courtyard was waiting for the music to begin. Candido took
his place in the middle with his clarinet. Every time he
pushed out his lips to start playing I liked watching his
face. He looked more serious than ever. A clarinet makes
a lovely sound and stands out above all the rest. Candido had a way of twisting the cord of the instrument
under his moustache and staring at the ground. He was
the leader of the band, too, conducting with his eyes.
All the time he was playing, nobody spoke a word. The
courtyard was filled with music. If anyone played a wrong
note Candido would shake his head, and raise his instrument towards the sky. Then everyone would stop playing.

That evening we ate as though this was a wedding
feast. I sat next to Candido. A woman there kept asking
him if I was his son, but everyone there knew how young
he was, and that all he really enjoyed was making music,
so they laughed at her. Another thing about Candido is
that he drinks very little. He advised me not to drink
because if I did I should not understand what was being
said. 'You must keep your head,' he often told me. 'You
have studies to do.' But I wanted to be gay, that night,
so I went on drinking in the courtyard as the others did,
coming out of the hot rooms into the cool air. We were all
drinking and eating grapes. I looked over at the dark
hill, where there was now not a single spark of fire. I felt
as if I'd been born in that courtyard and had been down
there with Candido ever since.

He noticed how sleepy I was and told me to go to bed. We argued a bit over this, but everyone told me the bed was ready and that I should soon get bored with watching the dancing. I replied that the dancing had nothing to do with it. I was just waiting for morning. Candido said I was quite right and a moment later they carried me to bed because what with hunger and exhaustion I was dead to the world.

Nudism

I went back to the torrent I had seen for the first time last winter. Now the weather was hot and, not surprisingly, the idea came into my head to strip off my clothes and go naked. Nothing but the trees and the birds could see me. The torrent gushed out from a cleft in the hillside and then flowed down between high banks. Everyone with a body at all knows what a good thing it is to expose it to the sky. Even the roots protruding from the high banks were bare.

I bathed in the pool where, fully extended, I could just touch bottom. The water was warm from its contact with the land and smelt of earth. Over and over again I plunged in, then threw myself down on the grass to let the sun burn me all over, while bright drops like sweat trickled over my skin. Above my head, between the tree tops, I could see the sky, looking like another empty pool. I stayed there until evening.

For several days, now, I've spent every afternoon naked in the sunshine, walking about on the grass, or at the edge of the pool. Sometimes, though very rarely indeed, when I throw myself dripping wet on the grass, I lose all consciousness of my body. This is nothing like the feeling of resentment and frustration I used to have, as a little boy, when I was made to undress and have a bath. Now I pull off my clothes in a mad rush, eager to find myself again and reappear, with a wildly beating heart. I was conscious, too, of a certain uneasiness lest something might happen to shatter my solitude, which means I should have to act as if prepared to be seen.

I'm not talking about people in general. On my way to the torrent I walked past fields where men and a few girls were busy with the harvest, but it was unthinkable that one of them might come upon me in this hollow in the ground, ringed around as it is by bushes and steep banks. I could hear the slightest movement of a quail or a lizard and so should always be warned in time to cover myself. My disquiet stemmed from a different cause and I found it not entirely devoid of pleasure. My state of complete nudity staggered and amazed me every time it happened, as if it were something of great importance I had achieved here unthinkingly. Every time I stretched out, remembering to cover the nape of my neck, I knew the sun had its eye on me, searching out every part of my body from head to foot. What difference is there between me and a stone, a tree trunk or a speckled caterpillar, unless it is precisely the mental disturbance I feel when considering the point. Now water and the sun have dealt with me to their liking and have thrown a veil over me. Even in this I seem to understand that nature will not tolerate human nudity and will do everything in its power to absorb the body as it does the dead. Sometimes I fancy I ought to stay in this place day and night. Instead, I go there every day and take off all my clothes, resisting the impulse yet at the same time exposing myself to the gaze of nature with as much pleasure as I can. Close by the pool is a hollow where the grass grows high, always marshy, always in the shade. I go there sometimes to look around. The grass grows up to my middle, my feet are in the mud, but coolness is not what I'm after. I go in there to hide and come out at some unexpected moment more naked than when I went in.

The shrill sound of birdsong above my head shows they are paying no attention to me whatsoever. Everything is going on as if I were not there at all. Looking upwards from the bottom of this hollow I see passing clouds and the way the treetops are rustling as if there were an abyss between them and myself. The wind doesn't reach me, down here. As soon as I have thrown myself down I forget the town and country places. My horizon has shrunk to the narrow limitations of the pool. Idly, but with amazement, I watch a butterfly or a tree trunk, as I feel with my body the pulsation of the earth on which I lie. At intervals the shadow of a cloud passes over me and then the air is cooler. Plants that are almost invisible in bright sunshine show up plainly like a tiny forest. They see their reflections in the water, the colours softened, yet distinguishable at a glance. Then I stand up and shake myself. I am bare as a tree trunk underneath its bark, cool and fresh as the air around me. I see the sky behind the trees is bare, too, bare and at peace.

The shadows increase and I look at the wood or the still water, but I cannot express what I see and think. The key words are 'grass' and 'roots', 'stones', 'mud'. The splendour of it all — no other word will do — but my body will not accept it. Enter into the grass, into a stone, my body says but that is not enough. This hollow in the ground has a nameless magic. To realise that this is so one must walk about in it, feel it, touch it. I have to make a real effort not to clutch at the roots and clamber up higher into the wood, between the thorny bushes and the green trunks, and walk about there. Instead, I content myself with discovering all I can about my own body.

It anyone were to come along when I've only just thrown myself down, dripping wet, I don't think I should bother to move. I'm as lazy as a block of wood. Water and sun working together, are making me less and less active. They imagine they can cancel me out in that way, cover me up, but they don't know that, instead, they're making me more and more like an animal. They harden my body so that it is capable of acting for itself. When I get here, covered in sweat, I am seized with the crazy idea of plastering myself all over with mud. I scoop it up in handfuls and rub it all over me. Then I lie in the sun till the mud has dried. (This, too, is a method of covering myself.) In this way, when I've washed it all off, I seem to come out of the water more naked than before.

Whenever the pool is stagnant and the water covered with slime, I'm content to strike out and reach clearer water, so that I come out clean. Somewhere below the surface there is a spring. The water from it is bitter and cold. I try to find it, rolling on my back in the mud or crouching like some toad under the big roots that over-hang the water. The slime quickly becomes mud and a whole afternoon is not long enough for it to clear again. One might say the sun concentrates his most ardent beams on this hollow. The pool looks to me like the sky during a heat wave. Now the water, being opaque, can no longer reflect anything. As I get out I still feel sweaty, with drops of water streaming down from my chest to my thighs.

After such bathes as this, the smell of swamp and mud is stronger. The hollow lies baking in the sunshine. There are rustlings, flutterings, a splash or two, and the song of birds. They seem to come from heaven knows where, but cannot be more than three paces away from me. It is at such a moment I forget I am naked. I close my eyes, and everything, the countryside, fruits, the steep banks, even a passer-by, should there be one, all from then on reveal their own personality, their existence and life beyond the trees. Everything has its own scent, its savour, its individuality. All this comes and goes inside my mind as I lie baking in the sun. Why should I move if someone were to come?

But nobody does come. Boredom does, though, indeed it does. I absorb the sunshine, the water; I wander about a bit and sit down on the grass, look around me and sniff. I go back to the water, but nothing ever happens. Little by little the shadow of a tree lengthens until it covers the place where I lie. A different freshness starts to fill the hollow, the stench of mud and of death increases. Now I can smell it as I smell my own body, which seems larger and more naked. Nobody comes, but why can't I go away?

The first time that whimsical thought occurred to me I felt terrified but I soon laughed myself out of that. Now, to rid myself of the taste and smell, I run up the path I came down to reach the pool, and stop between the low bushes where the grass is level. I am no longer

conscious of any barrier between myself and the countryside. Beyond the trees I can see the plain where the corn-
fields lie. I throw myself down on my back in the grass,
facing the sky and the last rays of the setting sun. I fear
no contact, not even with the stubble.

The harvest is finished now and the fields are deserted.
No matter which way I go, I never meet anyone. The
pool is waiting for me and I mourn for the days gone by.
The risk was well worth taking.

My mind turns to the people who bathe in the River
Po, especially to the women who imagine they are nude
when they have taken off their clothes and put on others.
Up and down they walk over cement or sand, making
signs to one another, glancing behind and chattering as
offensively as if they were in a drawing room. Then they
expose themselves to the sun, some of them slipping down
the straps from their shoulders to gain another hands-
breadth of sunburn. They all undress and look around
for their friends, but not one of them will put into words
what they all have in mind — that their bodies are very
different from those of other people. They have the courage
to congregate in groups but haven't the courage to do
what they'd all like to do.

During the past few days I've enjoyed strolling through
the fields under the eyes of men and women reapers and
their oxen. Good folk who don't concern themselves with
where I'm going. At any moment one of them could come
to my torrent to wash or to quench a thirst and discover
among the briars my body, burnt nearly black. Such
people as these, if they ever think of going for a bathe,

strip off their clothes without a moment's hesitation. Perhaps, though, they do not bathe unless they did so when they were boys. I walked close to the sheaves of corn and noticed the ears were dark brown, exactly matching my body. I watched the reapers stretch out their brown hands, and bend their backs, their red kerchiefs fluttering. All the uncovered parts of their bodies are the colour of tobacco. Their shirts and trousers are as earthy as the bark of a tree trunk. People like these have no need to go naked. They're naked already. As I walk among them the clothes I am wearing on my back seem to weigh me down. I feel as festive as an ox decked up for a parade. I wish they could know that underneath I'm as dark as they are.

It's happened! One woman at least knows my secret. I had gone into the water to wash off the earth clinging to me. I was floating on my back with my arms outstretched, looking up at the clear sky; my mind completely blank. I straightened up, slipping about on the muddy bottom and bent over to swill myself off when a woman walked across my hollow. She was tall, a married woman with a bundle of leafy boughs at her hip. She came towards me, not in the least surprised or concerned. She saw me bending forward, my hands in the water, then she turned away towards the ravine, still carrying her bundle. I heard her paddle through the water of a spring, then she disappeared among the bushes. Her feet were bare. I saw her strong back reappear in the sunshine between the bushes and I heard her gathering more branches further in.

She had come down the path I used when I ran to throw myself on the grass. She must have seen me from up there, yet she calmly continued on her way, not even giving a backward glance when she had passed by.

Standing upright in the water, naked, I listened to the sound of her footsteps dying away in the distance. I was certainly more shocked than she was. Drops of water were running down from my skin. I went out to dry myself and I still couldn't believe it had really happened. How was it that I hadn't heard her coming? A woman's steps are different from a man's, but I wasn't thinking of that just then. I was thinking of the way she had looked at me, without a blush or any curiosity, as if it was a natural thing to happen. If she had paused, or spoken to me with a smile, that would have been very different. I should have covered myself and perhaps even touched her. In either case I should not have been so agitated. Yet she was young, for in this part of the world, wives lose their beauty early.

The chill of evening was falling and I felt even more naked. My thoughts turned to that woman's eyes. She was sunburned, too. Was she tanned all over? Certainly she had no need to be. That isn't what matters. What is really important for her is to be healthy and to produce fine strong children. She gets as much sunshine as she wants while walking about in the open air. The same sun ripens the fields and the fruit, for here everyone drinks wine. Grapes darken, even when covered by leaves. The important thing to realise is that underneath there is corporal identity.

She wore a dark coloured skirt around her strong legs and she walked heedless of stones or trailing roots. I can still see her striding purposefully into the wood to gather branches from the acacia trees that grow in such profusion there. They overhang the steep sides of the ravine and thrust out their roots. To me it seems they are peering down into the underworld and up to the sky. This is a hidden part of the wood, appealing to the senses with its dark shadows, its gloomy depths. By now the woman must be far away from here. Before me I see a bare ledge of veined stone that tells me the wood has its own individuality as the whole countryside has, covered with earth that in its turn is covered with growing things, naked and true to itself, as we all are. I touch my skin that still retains the warmth of the sun and I feel glad the woman saw me.

On my way home I pause for a chat at the crossroads where there is nearly always someone ready to talk. Yesterday I saw Marchino and told him where I'd been. 'I should go bathing there, too,' he remarked. He's a sad-looking man with two fingers length of beard and hard eyes, but courteous enough not to ask if he could come with me. He told me that tomorrow he was planning to go swimming at a place he knew where a mill stream broadens out to form a lake and there is always running water. 'If you'd like to come . . . ?' he suggested. I raised the difficult point that I don't wear bathing trunks. 'You know best,' he replied. 'With me there's no need to.'

That same evening we went to the place he had told me about, where the channel broadens out into a lake with banks of gravel and willow branches beaten down by the sun. At this time of day the boys are all in the fields.

We took off our clothes and put them down in a patch of shade, then entered the water. It was silvery and caressing, though full of sand. Marchino swam with powerful strokes, while I stayed where I was, floating and looking up at the sky. In those few moments I was still thinking of the countryside, the treetops and the life that goes on up there.

When we came out of the water I had a better chance to look at Marchino. He must have been half-naked while working at the harvest this season, for the only pale skin he had was on his stomach and thighs. He was hairy, covered with fine blond hairs bleached by the dog-days of summer. He was perfectly calm as he walked up the bank and flung himself full length on the sand. I turned my gaze away from him.

Between one subject of conversation and another we went back to the water to cool our heads. Marchino left it to me to talk of this and that, and he would reply at his own convenience after a while. Sometimes he spoke when I was already thinking of something else. I was pleased by the knotted muscles of his chest that didn't move, not even when he took a deep breath.

He remarked that I must have spent a lot of time sunbathing to be so dark, almost black. 'I didn't get it while working,' I replied, 'I'd rather be you than me, getting it that way. It's important to be tanned all over. Otherwise what a figure of fun you'd look on some special occasion!' We were talking idly, resting our necks on little cushions of sand. After a while he agreed with me and saw the funny side of it. He thought for another minute or two, and went on : 'When they reach that point it's not our sunburn they're thinking of.'

In my mind's eye I was watching the woman as she

came through the wood. The thought struck me that
Marchino would have been an ideal match for her. I
felt inclined to tell him so, but how could I? Marchino
would not have understood. It's typical of him not to think
of things like that.

Approaching my hollow, I came between the trees above
the ravine in the warm dusk, treading the path the woman
had taken, walking cautiously. Any country place is far
from being simple. Just think how many people must
have come this way to create such a path. Every bank
of the stream, every spot in the wood, must have seen
something. Every place has a name of its own.

Through gaps in the leaves, like little windows, I look
up to the sky. Below it stands the hill and the level ground,
both with their carpet of fields. Their gentle sweetness
bears a hint of work and sweat, an atmosphere that en-
folds the whole wood and the uncultivated corners it
contains, betraying their nakedness. Here, in such places
as these, often marked by a thicket or a special stone,
the land lies naked and unconcealed.

I paused for a moment on the fringe of the trees. This
is where cultivation begins and the hard work it entails.
A few clumps of acacia and alder, hanging above the
cleft where the torrent begins, give the scene a wild, uncultivated air. I cannot go farther in, since I am naked.
This time I understand why, to undress, one must go down
to the little clearing beside the stream; also why country
folk wear clothes when they go into the fields to work
and to cultivate the land.

This is why the woman looked at me so calmly. She

knew I was hidden, a luxury in itself. To see my body was much the same as seeing her own. She didn't know I was thinking of going out to the fields. Everything in the country has a name, but there is no name for a gesture like that. And neither she nor Marchino gave it a thought.

By this time the sun was setting, even in this place. I heard the grass waving about, making a rustling sound. Birds fly past; a deeper murmur lulls earth and sky. The land seems bare, but is not. Everywhere mists are rising, to cover and retain the smell of sweat. I wonder whether there is, in the whole world, a ditch, a coastline, a little patch of earth not yet dug up and reshaped by men's hands. Everything bears the stamp of human observation, human management. It comes from the fields like a gentle breath, but does not reach my hollow, where water, liquid mud and the smell of sweat stagnate all together and have no other message for me. Yet every day I find a new life there, as I lie fully extended, like a dead man, my skin burnt almost black.

Told in Confidence

This is the track my father used to follow, walking all through the night so as to arrive early. He would climb the first hill, cross the wide valley, then make his way over the other hills until he and the rising sun met face to face on the final crest. The path wound upwards to the bank of clouds that rolled away as the first sunbeams shone through. Below was a layer of smoky fog rising from the plain. I've seen those clouds myself, shining like gold. In my father's day he used to say that when they were low and fiery red the coming day would be fine. Then gold pieces changed hands more freely in the market place.

Even nowadays, traders on foot can be seen making their way down towards level ground, leaning forward, with their cloaks covering their mouths. They never look round, not even on a fine day. Their shadows fall behind them on the road, quietly following them. The hill lies behind them, too, with its level skyline. I know that skyline and every one of the stunted trees that crown the hilltop. I also know what things can be seen from those trees.

My father didn't go down to the plain at daybreak. First he would visit hillside farms, displaying the goods he had for sale and talking to sleepy people in the farmyards. They shared a meal and then had a drink on the doorstep in almost complete silence. My father knew everybody, and also he knew the owner of every farm building by the roadside. He was on good terms with these people and was well aware of their troubles, their disappointments, their needs, their women. He never had much to say. If other pedlars were present he would let them go on talking, but hardly ever put in a word himself.

Many years ago, when he was left a widower and we children were just babies, someone advised him to give up what he had been doing and set himself up in business with a horse and cart for hire, but it was wintertime and he decided a horse would find it hard work on those steep and narrow lanes. So, wearing a fur cap and muffled up to his eyes, he would start off through the mists to get as far as Bicocca, two valleys away. This property consisted of a farmhouse and surrounding land. Sandiana lived there then. She was the daughter of a friend of his, still young but despondent ever since her father's death had left her to look after the vineyard by herself. My father had it in mind to bring her home with him and beget another son, but she would spend the whole day huddled over the fire in a room as filthy as a henhouse, moaning all the time that she was lonely and frightened.

One day he heard a rumour that a man living outside our village was thinking of giving up working as a pedlar and retiring to live quietly in town. My father wondered what truth there was in this bit of gossip, and tramped over there through deep snow to find out. Till then my father had no idea there might be land for sale. Everybody living in the neighbourhood wanted to buy some. One day he reached Bicocca to find another man toasting his feet by the fire, and when he arrived home he found that fellow's sons loading up our household goods and carting them off to Bicocca. That was the first time he realised he was getting old. Sandiana went off to live near the market.

He never discussed things like that with us. Local people had a general impression that he spent those years hunting. By now Sandiana had gone street-walking in the town so often that she was getting a bad name there. The place where she lived had a little low courtyard covered in with new vines. The noise from the market hardly reached her there. The trader who had sold his land had gone back where he came from. Sandiana still waited, huddled close to the fire like a cat. For a long time my father had a hot meal sent in to her every day. She spent the winter there, sitting watching the comings and goings in the street outside, the eddies of smoke, the market traders. Sometimes she seemed to be listening to everything they said. Any affairs she ought to have seen to, she left to be dealt with by other people. She was still dreaming of that vineyard.

All that winter she never went outside the courtyard. Having now no land of her own she knew she was worth nothing, and she was pregnant into the bargain. She quarrelled with the woman who brought her food and grumbled that old men were worse than young ones. She sent my father a message that she intended to kill herself. My father let that winter go by, then started tramping the hills again. In March he heard she'd had her baby and went to see her, renewing his offer to take her home with him. People said she was now very thin and always in floods of tears. I know my father had to tell her straight that he'd brought her into our home to see to things a woman normally did, in a house that lacked a mistress. She was not mistress here, not even servant. We weren't all that well off.

So he set aside a room for Sandiana and her baby, continuing to sleep alone himself. His idea of fathering another son fell into the background, now he had the vineyard. Not even in the summer did my father change his mind, though Sandiana blossomed like a happy wife and mother as she fed her baby at the breast. My father left home before daylight and she would get up to prepare food for him to take. They hardly ever exchanged a word. We boys, put up to it by the servant, strained our ears to catch anything we could. We all liked Sandiana. She looked after us and helped us.

Towards evening, in summer time, we would go walking with her in the country round about. We knew the way father would take on his way home and we kept a good lookout, each of us hoping to be the first to get a glimpse of him up on the hilltop. We took Sandiana to see our favourite vantage points and she could tell us the names of all the bell-towers and villages we could see, no matter how far away. She told us all about what could be seen of the plain from a viewpoint just beyond certain clumps of trees, and what people would be doing in various little isolated cottages. She also talked to us of her own father, and of what she and her numerous brothers and sisters used to do when they lived at Bicocca. Every evening they would go round, carrying lanterns, to shut up the stables, henhouses and cellars. She described the time when her grandparents heard a wolf scratching at their door one winter's night but they went on weaving baskets and kept a good lookout. There was a game we played, each of us choosing a different path through the vineyards. Whoever reached the top first would give a shout and wave his arms against the sky. She was a good runner, too.

During the past year I had grown a lot and arrangements had been made for me to spend the winter at a school in the city. Sandiana told me this would be good for me. She added that I'd quickly forget what it was like to live in the country. I should soon feel ashamed of my home and my family, and I knew she was right. Though summer was nearly over, I at once started looking intently at the streets, the clouds, the grapes, to stamp them indelibly in my memory, so that later on I could talk about it all. I wished I had been born at Bicocca, among Sandiana's old folk. I wished I had known her brothers and discovered for myself the thrill of the nights when the wolves came. How I would have bragged about that! Listening to Sandiana's voice I realised she knew I would. From then on I became aware that what gave me the most pleasure was not the things I did myself, but what I heard about from other people. I wasn't like my father any longer.

Sandiana's old home was now in the hands of an elderly couple, under a business arrangement with a gentleman who had bought the place, but no one knew who he was. We often climbed up that hill. From it we could see the pine trees, black beyond the far side of the house. They grew very tall, standing out among the vines like towers, alive with birds. One day she took us as far as the yard. A dog there recognised her and came running to welcome her, jumping up against her back. An old woman came out and talked with her, then they went round together looking over the house and the threshing floor. We waited for them in the courtyard under the shade of a stack of straw, throwing stones at the tallest pine tree. I had never been in such an empty farmyard. It looked deserted, left to rack and ruin.

Even the dog I could hear yelping up there with the
women was one I had never seen. Its voice sounded
fiercer than the bark of an ordinary dog. At the time I
thought that Sandiana's brothers must be circling the
woods on the far side of the hill. When the old woman
and Sandiana came back they were both bemoaning
something they didn't like. The old woman said she'd like
to give us something — a quince perhaps — but she couldn't
find any. Sandiana was smiling, quite content.

The dog wanted to come with us and had to be put on
a leash. Going home we went a different way and Sandiana didn't say a word, except to advise us not to mention
to my father that we'd gone to the house. He'd say it was
too far. That evening she asked me if I knew whether
my father had gone up there this summer. I replied that
she should have asked the old woman that question,
and she said no more.

One morning we found father in the kitchen. It wasn't
Sunday, but everything had an air of unreality. Sandiana
came back from the yards looking distracted with her hair
over her eyes. The baby was crying, so the maid was sent
to pacify him. My father was giving orders and making
jokes. The day I was to go away to school hadn't yet
come and I didn't know what all the fuss was about, but
then the maid dropped a hint. Bicocca now belonged to
us. My father had bought it.

Off they went in a hired cab, father and Sandiana. On
that day our little servant girl was in a spiteful mood. She
told us, just as if we were grown men, that from now on
Sandiana would be mistress of the house and Bicocca
would belong to her and her son. We waited all day for
them to come home. I thought Sandiana might at least
let me wander about in the wood I had seen at Bicocca

and so as to deserve it I helped look after the baby. The servant told me that from now on he was my brother. That made me think, more than anything else, of my brothers who had died. I was glad to know they had been my brothers, too. That evening the servant told my father that today's events called for a celebration, and went off to bring some wine.

So many years have passed since then and there are more to come. I went to the city and changed my way of life. I went home a year later, but I had become a different person. I came to spend my holidays in the country, so it seemed to me I was a boy again only in the summer. Sandiana was still the same. Her baby had died and life in our house hardly seemed to move at all. Every year the summer was to me just as it had been before I went away, a holiday that would last for ever.

Every year, I watched the clouds, the grapes and the crops so that I could talk about them in the city, but, I don't know how it happened, my thoughts when I was there turned to other matters and I never spoke of them. Sandiana was right. She was always asking whether the boys I was with at school ever poked fun at me, and if I would come back again to work in the vineyard. When I did so I felt happy and asked her if she'd like to come too. Whenever I came home from my school in the city, on that same day I would walk along every road, every path in the neighbourhood. When I woke next morning I felt happy if the sun was shining, happier still if it was raining, for there's nothing like rain to inspire a longing for a country walk.

If I came home wet through and covered in mud, Sandiana laughed and said she would have come with me, at one time.

She didn't come, but one evening we were caught in a thunderstorm out in the street. We boys were afraid of the thunder, Sandiana of the lightning. I like the lightning, that unexpected violet light flooding over us like water, but Sandiana told us that it was sulphurous and that it killed people by shock. 'It's nothing,' I replied, 'just a light going by.' 'You don't know,' she retorted. 'Whatever it touches, it kills.' I sniffed at the drenched air and smelled at last the odour of the lightning. A new smell, like that of a flower one has never seen before, crashing between the clouds and the water.

'Can you smell it?' I asked her. But Sandiana was holding her hands tightly over her ears in the doorway where we had taken shelter. The perfume stayed with us till we reached home. It was fresh and cool, causing a prickly feeling inside one's nostrils, like one gets when plunging one's face into a basin of water. Sandiana said the perfume was there because the wind had just blown over the wood, but I had never smelt it before. It was in very truth the smell of lightning. 'Who can tell where it struck?' she said, but would not come with me to look for the place. 'It must have come down in the woods,' she insisted. She knew too much about woodcraft. Now I understood why so many strange stories are told about woods. There are so many growing things there, so many flowers one has never seen before, the sounds of little creatures hiding in the bushes. Perhaps the lightning has changed into a stone, a lizard, a bank of lovely little flowers. One can only tell by the smell.

Certainly there were patches of burnt earth, but the

smell of them no longer held any trace of the smell of water, in my opinion, though Sandiana didn't agree with me.

Deep in the woods near Bicocca there was a cleft in the rocks, that Sandiana told me had been caused by an earth tremor, long before either of us was born. Nothing but a lizard could manage to cross it. However, I had once seen a lovely lilac tree blossoming up there and I wondered whether its perfume was like the smell of lightning. Who can say? I understood that thunder can split the earth, but a storm of rain comes from heaven and so can bring with it nothing but good.

'But,' said Sandiana, 'every living thing comes from the earth. Everything is made of earth. Deep in the ground are roots and water. All the goodness in the grain you eat and the wine from grapes comes from the ground.'

I had never thought about the earth having a part to play in forming the grain and keeping it in good heart. It struck me all the more forcibly now that I had become a student. We owned Bicocca, but that didn't mean we were ordinary country folk. However, when I tasted the fruit grown there I understood what she meant.

Fruit has many different flavours, depending on where it was grown. One gets to know them as if they were people. There are thin ones, strong and healthy ones, some are bad, others taste harsh and bitter. Now and again you may come across one that has to be pampered like a girl. There are fig-trees at Bicocca and the sort of grapes that ripen in July. They still have something about them that brings Sandiana to mind. I have eaten every kind of fruit that grows wild, including medlars and sloes — the fruit of the blackthorn. Best of all I like sloes and can smell them a long way off. The bushes have sharp spikes and grow along the edge of uncultivated land or among brambles, where their vivid green colour stands out brightly. By the end of August their branches are thick with dark blue berries, a much darker blue than the sky, growing in tight clusters. They have a harsh bitter taste that most people dislike. One good thing about them is that by November all the berries will have fallen off.

Blackthorns know how to choose good, hitherto undisturbed earth. That much is clear from the places where they grow. I always used to find them around the edges of vineyards, where cultivation ends and nothing else will grow. Beyond them there is only the dry barren soil of land that has been cleared. At that time I didn't think about such things. I simply wished that my father, Sandiana and everybody else would eat sloes. I don't know about other people, but Sandiana said they bit her tongue. 'That's what I like about them,' I said. 'The very smell of them shows they grow in the wild. Nobody touches them, yet they come up. If the land were left to itself there would be still more blackthorns.'

Sandiana laughed and said to me, 'Do you know. . . .'

'Know what?' But she wouldn't say any more just then.

One day she told me that beyond the woods where she had been living, there was a valley. If one crossed it and walked up the other side, one would eventually come to a place called Madonna della Rovere where one could see that all along the coast lay a dense growth of blackthorn.

'Can we go there?' I asked.

'It's too far away.'

'Don't people living there gather the sloes?'

I turned this over in my mind for a long time. I wanted to know more about it. What I had been told was not enough. There was so much to discover about our roads, how many hills there were in the world, how much land was being allowed to run to waste, with blackthorn bushes growing everywhere, all along the river banks and in ditches, in places so inaccessible that no man could ever penetrate, even if he wanted to. I pictured to myself their crinkled leaves, their little branches loaded with fruit, calmly waiting for the hand of a reaper who would never come. Even today it seems to me absurd to squander so many tasty flavours, so many appetising juices no one will ever enjoy. We reap our corn, we harvest our grapes, but it's never enough. The richness of our soil is shown by the plants that grow wild. Not even the birds, country creatures as they are, can enjoy them, because the prickles hurt their eyes.

I thought over these things and about the creatures that live in these woods, the rich flavours, the passing clouds. Sandiana must have watched them when she was living up here beside the trees. I realised that all was not yet lost. With some things it is enough to know they exist and be thankful for them. 'One cannot eat more than one or two sloes at a time,' Sandiana remarked, 'but it's nice to know they grow everywhere.'

By this time it was enough for someone to mention any country place and I could picture it at once. All villages have dairy farms, reed-beds and fields of growing crops, as ours does. I seemed to have been there, or would be going tomorrow. Nobody ever forced their way into those dense thickets, yet when my father was driving up with his horse and cart, taking me with him, I would start off on a tour of exploration. Deep in the woods there were things he knew nothing of, things that to me were more important than anything else.

A road and a reed-bed are common enough, at least to us they are, but catching a glimpse of them in the distance, under the ridge of a high hill, and knowing that beyond them there are other hills, other reed-beds, made me think. No matter how far I went, there would always remain places I hadn't yet visited. Somebody had been there, but not me. These were the thoughts running through my head as I listened to Sandiana. I envied my father who had travelled to so many places and had walked along those paths and climbed those hills by day and by night. Not until later did I realise how exhausting it was. At that period I was quite content to watch him come home in the evening and drag himself wearily up three flights of stairs without saying a word or waiting for the rest of us to come in. At such a moment he didn't look like my father any more. One glance at his face showed he had come a long way and was tired out — though his eyes still held their characteristic gleam of independence. He was so exhausted that, if Sandiana called him he would go to her, not having enough strength left to utter a single word. They never discussed any country affairs between themselves.

Sometimes he would take us for a drive, only a short one, though, because the horse was already tired from pulling him about all day, even though there was nobody else in the cart. So we went for longer and longer walks. Once at the beginning of summer and once at the end my father would take me with him along the main road to the town. As he drove, I was thinking of the days when Sandiana was living up there on the hill. It seemed to

me a long time ago. I hadn't even seen the town then.
I asked my father if it was true that when he was a boy
he had run away from home, secretly. He replied somewhat brusquely, yet jokingly, not answering my question.
Instead he said : 'The Madonna of the Oaktrees? Only
elderly people bother to go there now, just to see the
festivities. Then they walk home through the night.'
Young lads had been left in charge of everything, and
had spent the time seeing how many toads they could
catch and watching the reflections of light in the distance.
'Nowadays,' my father said, 'people have great houses
like palaces and look down on country folk like us. They
amuse themselves behind closed doors. It isn't worth the
trouble of coming here any more.'

In the fresh cool light of dawn I kept a good lookout
to see for myself where the main road ended and the
palaces began. Everywhere there was a mist tinged with
gold. It seemed as if the air we breathed was different
down here. Little by little it filled our lungs, and by the
time we reached the town itself it seemed impossible to
believe that such things as hills and country villages still
existed. Far away — who knows where — lay the sea. I
told my father what I was thinking and he gave a short
brusque laugh.

Now time has gone by and I look back on those summers, I know what it was I wanted from the Madonna
of the Oak Trees. A blackthorn hedge cut off my view
of the horizon when I liked to watch the clouds drifting
past, catching glimpses of roads and far away places. But
it's enough to know they exist. The Oaktree Madonna has
existed from time immemorial. Everywhere along the
coast and up above the villages there are churches in
her honour, backed by masses of trees that, seen from a

distance, look stunted, though they are not really so. Inside the churches the light has colour and the sky is quiet and serene. Women like Sandiana spend hours kneeling there, crossing themselves. There is always at least one woman on her knees in the church. If a ventilator in the roof has been opened, one is aware of a warmer breath of air coming straight from heaven and a reminder that outside the church there are living things, plants growing wild, for instance, each with its own taste and smell.

These hillside churches are all alike. There is always another farther on that one has never seen. Their pillared porches are roofed in by the sky. Standing there I could smell the perfume of blackthorn bushes and reed-beds, though I had not walked far enough to reach them. How rewarding it is to stop now and then and look closely at everything there is to be seen within a couple of paces, and learn that the whole world is one vast forest we can never make truly our own, as we can with fruit. The little plants growing at our feet have their own earth smell, their own taste. If it is true that fields and vineyards nourish each other, it is because their roots can exert a hidden power. My father used to tell me that everything in the world grows from the bottom upwards. I don't know even now, nor did I then, whether this is true. To me, the church of the Oaktree Madonna was like a sanctuary for little hidden, far away plants that had to find some way to go on living.

When my father died, some years ago now, I found in my grief a kind of calm serenity I had not expected, though I had always known of it. I went to the church and to the cemetery; I took another look at the women wearing veils on their heads and at the little paintings of

the *Via Crucis*. There was a smell of incense and of
freshly dug earth. Sandiana, more upset than I was,
prayed over his grave. Then we went back home together
and she began preparing supper. It was a long time before
I turned round. The courtyard seemed smaller. We talked
about my father and about Bicocca, the harvest and death.
Then I stayed alone by the window till the night was far
advanced.

In those days I thought over many things I had forgotten. I thought about my father, now existing as part
of the untamed woodland. There was no longer any need
for him to travel round all day and all night to tell me
so. The church, as was right and proper, had swallowed
him up, but the church itself cannot move, cannot go
beyond the horizon. My father now lay underground but
had not changed. His body and blood would create roots
to join the thousand others left there when plants
have been cut down. These roots exist. The earth is
full of them. The stained glass windows in the church do
nothing to change them. Indeed they make us realise
that nothing ever does change, not even outside under the
sky. No matter how far away or deeply buried, everything goes on living quietly in that calm and gentle light.

Now, in everything around me I was conscious of my
father's presence. My bitter, constant grief for his absence
had its effect on everything I saw, every voice I heard in
the countryside. I could never remember him as he lay
in his narrow coffin.

Every village around here has its own churches and
chapels. I visited them in turn, well aware he was with me
wherever I went. He walked ahead of me over the steepest
hills as if I were a boy again. In places that seemed to
me particularly his own I would pause a minute or two

for his sake, feeling I was actually a boy again. At day-break I would try to see the road and the town in the valley below, still shrouded in mist, where — How long ago? — he had arrived one morning with the purposeful, steady stride of a country-born young man.

We talked about him. When Sandiana was just a baby, she had watched him dancing and knew how his voice sounded then. She told me that instead of lending a hand with the farm work he preferred to travel the roads, buying and selling horses. He liked doing business, but even more he liked wandering round the country. He had certainly seen a great many places. He had met our mother in the town and married her without telling anyone about it. Then he went back to the country and made his peace with his neighbours by inviting them to a grand wedding banquet. My eldest sister was born two days later.

In those days my father was lighthearted and quick-tempered. Sandiana told me that when he was forty he teamed up with his brothers and went round with them playing jokes on people like a young hooligan. They were always to be seen at Bicocca, but she was surprised that he had married. My mother would come looking for him if they stayed out late at night. She was young and always looked frightened. Beside him, she could have been taken for his daughter. Whoever would have thought she would be the first to die? Sandiana had forgotten we were talking of my father, and began telling me about the women and their families.

I fell silent, seeing again in my mind the city in fog. This wasn't what I was seeking from her. Women had made my father what he was, but there was something more than that, something that had happened long ago, something secret to be buried and forgotten for ever. I mean a child.

Like myself, my father had gone to the town, not to be shut up in a school, but to make his fortune. He went there as a rustic and did not change. I wondered what he had been trying to find up there, what fury, what instinct moved him — a man who had been born in a field. The sleeping city had seemed superb to him in the end. He had never settled down there, but his women came up to seek him out, even the last of them, the one from Bicocca. Perhaps he had known all about it from the beginning. Perhaps, too, he was trying to find something quite unknown there — the spirit of fields and forests.

At this point I turned to Sandiana and asked her whether my father had ever thought of settling down in the city. Apparently she didn't understand what lay behind my question and said in that case he wouldn't have bought Bicocca. Actually she understood me very well. Here is her reply.

My father liked going down into town straight from the fields. His real work was done on a threshing floor and he would travel from one of them to another all round the neighbourhood, earning good money. To him, palatial houses and markets stood for gold pieces, cart-loads of sacks and bundles of odds and ends he had acquired. He couldn't be sure whether or not some of his workmates were country lads who had come into town to find a job, as he had done himself. With others he was always laughing and cracking jokes. That's what he was like as a lad, and that's why he had died.

Now there was no longer any point in climbing the hills to feel alone with him. It was quite enough to move me deeply if I came across a reed-bed or a stunted fig-tree out-

lined against the sky, or a patch of freshly dug earth.
Yet in a way it was satisfying. Anything far off, beyond
the hills, the town, the smoky plain, once buried, was nothing more than a church shut off from the horizon by
clumps of trees.

By contrast, the geraniums Sandiana grew in her
windowbox seemed citified to me. Their brilliant colours
are rivalled only by poppies, but their leaves and their
intricate shapes show plainly that they are not growing
in the earth itself. Very soon I should see masses of
them in the low-lying fields and balconies in the town.
When I watched Sandiana at the window watering them
it seemed to me there was something about her I had
never seen before, and she was as red as her flowers.
Sandiana seemed to me a stranger. Everything she did
had something new and different about it, all the more
since I now only saw her in the summer. When we went
to Bicocca I followed her everywhere, into the main rooms
furnished with dark red hangings, up to the garrets, in
front of the windows. Ranged along the wall there were
massive storage chests, always kept shut. The brick floors
were covered with corn, potatoes and maize, so that we
had to take off our shoes to cross the room. Sandiana
went around, touching things and looking at them. 'Who
knows how cold these rooms are in winter?' I remarked.
'It's cold everywhere in winter,' she said sharply. The
house might have belonged to someone else and it was as
if she had come back there out of curiosity, to learn more
about it. She was happy, that much was clear.

'You see,' she said, 'your father bought all this for you
and the others.' We had hardly reached the place when
she filled a bucket of water from the well and took it
into the kitchen. As if the men of the house were out in

the fields haymaking or something, she tied a kerchief
over her head and went out too. I strolled up along the
paths to look for sloes growing around the vines. From
where I stood I could see there was movement in the
middle of the field, and it seemed a good idea to hide
myself in that quiet place, in the uncultivated land under
the last row of vines, only a step or two from the wood.
Then terror seized me and I rushed down the path at
breakneck speed. Seeing me running, the people in the
field all burst out laughing. 'Run!' they were saying.
'Panic has gripped you!'

Fear is something that exists for everybody. Sandiana
told me I should have put up some resistance. 'If you
stand your ground,' she told me, 'you can overcome
panic, but if you run away it will creep up behind you
like a wind in the night.' 'It scared me in broad daylight,'
I told her.

'If there's daylight,' she said, 'the thing to do is to stare
at it straight between the eyes. Then it will run away
and hide.'

The mere idea of out-facing whatever it was that
frightened me was even more terrifying. 'Have you seen
it?' I asked her. 'What's it like?'

'You've felt it yourself.'

'No I haven't.'

Sandiana was laughing. 'Then you must pay more
attention if it happens again.'

Talking on these lines worked me up to a pitch of
excitement. 'It isn't only fear,' I said. 'When I'm by
myself in the vineyard or the porch I get the feeling I'm
waiting for something to happen, something that's bound
to happen soon. Sometimes I go there on purpose. If I
hadn't run away I would have seen what it was like.'

'You should have stayed there,' she said.

'It's something like the feeling one gets when one throws a piece of iron through a window, just for fun. Above a dying fire the air seems to quiver as if the sky were trembling. Have you ever seen that?'

'Yes.'

'Have you ever seen that sort of thing out in the country?'

'Oh yes!'

'No. You're laughing at me. It seems to me that steady currents of warm air are always coming up from the earth. They keep plants green and make them grow. There are days when I get the feeling that if I go walking, no matter where I set my feet, something alive underground is aware of it. When the sun is stronger you can hear a rumble from the earth as it grows.'

Never before had I confided these thoughts of mine to anyone. Sandiana said I was quite right, and went on to tell me that she once had a flower that opened every morning when the first sunbeam shone. It moved by itself, too.

'Are there any like that in the woods now?' I asked her.

'Who can tell?' she replied. 'There's everything in the woods.'

We sometimes went into the woods to gather mushrooms, provided there had been rain. Sandiana gathered more than all the rest of us put together. She knew every inch of the ground, and would put her hand under the withered leaves and was never once wrong. Sometimes I would pass her and look back, but she had nobody with her. When she came, it seemed as if they sprang up at her feet. With a smile she told me that mushrooms grew all of a sudden, between night and morning, even between one hour and the next. They knew her hand, she said. They're like moles and can move about. They're produced by water and warmth. It was a pity the place was so far away. I couldn't go there except with her. We would leave the house early in the morning and were drenched with sweat by the time we had reached the crest of the hill. Then we had to cross a valley and the slopes beyond, with no paths to guide us. On those nights as I lay in bed, it seemed to me the hill must be one huge hotbed of rain and mushrooms. No one but Sandiana could find the place, but she knew it like the back of her hand.

'My grandfather used to say,' she remarked to me one day, 'that all the labour you put into working on the land all day is poured back into your blood during the night. There's something special about the soil up there. You breathe it in while you sweat. He said, too, that it's much less tiring to walk on our own land than on a road. He was very old and I never knew much about him.'

'What did he mean by that bit about a road?' I asked, though I felt I already knew. Sandiana looked at me keenly, as if she thought I was pulling her leg. 'Why?' she said, 'because you don't have to cultivate a road.'

'All the same, a road is part of the land,' I said.

'You'd better go and ask him, then,' she retorted.

At Bicocca, just behind the house, stood a cliff of porous stone where somebody (probably Sandiana's grandfather, I thought) had dug out a cavern so deep that it had an echo. Inside it there were tools and farm implements, carts and piles of rubbish. With the passing of time the rocky walls had turned grey, but at the back, where it was darker, the air felt clammy and there was a little spring. Maidenhair ferns were growing there in great profusion. Country girls consider them very pretty. Sandiana went there once to cut enough to fill a vase. I held the candle for her.

'We're right under the hill, just here,' I said.

'It's cooler here than it was on top.'

All the time we stayed underground I was thinking of her grandfather. 'Water must be the sweat given off by the roots,' I said, but I said it to myself, so that Sandiana wouldn't be able to tease me about it. I couldn't resist asking her whether geraniums like hers would grow underground.

'You're mad,' she cried. 'Why do you ask?'

'They're alike.'

'How?'

'They won't grow underground, nor will they grow wild anywhere in the country.'

'Aren't we in the country?'

Then I realised it was no good trying to tell her anything. True enough, the word 'country' doesn't mean merely the topsoil but everything inside it as well. A wish occurred to me. How I should like to stay down here one evening until the next morning! If there was rain in the night it would make the trees grow. 'It's nearly dark in here already,' I thought, 'but underground it's dark all the time.'

Once or twice I came here alone, but, as always happens when I'm somewhere really quiet, I found I was straining my ears to catch the slightest sound. At the entrance I turned back to look into the darkness. I fancied I could hear water gurgling as it trickled from the rock-face, moistening the vault and permeating the whole hill. My thoughts were with that fine old man trudging along the paths he knew so well. He must certainly have known, better than anybody else, the secrets of the countryside, but now he was dead and buried. I took one more step forward and found myself in the yard with the sky above me.

My talks with Sandiana took place at the time when everybody else was enjoying a siesta, between lunch and tea, while outside the sun was blazing fiercely down. I would go out for a stroll between the houses, out into the dazzling whiteness, and I still remember the thoughts that came to me then. I was feeling irritated and waited impatiently for the time when the ordinary daily life would start again. My bad temper reached the peak typical of long working days and summer heat. There was nothing to be heard, not even the sound of a voice in the yard or on the slopes beyond. This emptiness fascinated me. It was as if time itself had ceased.

I had reached the stage when everything seemed possible and permissible, though I couldn't understand why, with such activity going on around me, everything had suddenly gone quiet. I looked down at the ants on the ground, then over to the distant trees, tiny against the broad sweep of the hill. The ants seemed restless. Even the trees looked limp, exhausted by the heat.

Sometimes on my way home I would turn aside and go up to see if she was at the window where her geraniums grew. Between those flowers and the hilltops, whitened by the sun till they looked like lime, there was hidden treasure. I felt sure of that. I gazed from the flowers up to the hills, hardly knowing why I did so. I hadn't mentioned my ideas to Sandiana. She would only have poked fun at me. It suited my purpose, rather than hers, to talk through an open window. Many a time I looked

at her as impersonally as I did at the geraniums bloom-
ing in the city. She had done the same in her day.

The town had a wealth of little byways, where great
doors would sometimes swing open to reveal unexpected
gardens. I used to catch a glimpse of them on the way
to school, thinking the earth must be different there,
more secret, more lovely than ours. I was certain that
my father had never even glanced inside so I didn't
venture to ask him about them. But I knew that Sandiana
had at one time lived among those lanes and must have
known them well. I tried to find out all I could about her
life as a young girl, and why, in winter, her face was
redder than fire. Neither my father nor I ever mentioned
it to her. Who she had caught it from I have no idea. I
never set foot in those courtyards and was quite content to
walk past them. When I heard there was a vine growing
there I wondered why Sandiana hadn't stayed. I tried
to imagine what it would be like if we went there together
now, climbed the wide dignified staircases and spent a
little while in that palatial house.

My father and Sandiana both came to see me once or
twice at school during the winter, on Sundays. I had
permission to go out with them, with her, but I couldn't
bring myself to tell them what life in the town was like.
They took me to the market place, where my father
ordered tea. He would spend some time chatting to the
proprietor, while the rest of us went out to watch the
people passing by. We walked along the stretch of road
between the entrance of the café and the castle. There
were well-dressed ladies and gentlemen, soldiers and boys
like me, only much better off, all strolling about at their
leisure, stopping a while, turning round, making signs to
one another or shouting. Standing in the cold outside the

café I was quite fascinated by the smoke inside, glinting here and there, but Sandiana would take my hand, feeling anxious if I seemed tired and taking care of me until, torn between curiosity and impatience, she had seen all there was to see.

I much preferred the times when she had something else to do. Then we would make our way through the crowds and run along the deserted lanes where my gardens had been. The weather was cold now, but I could always tell her what flowers grew there in season. I asked who lived in palaces like that and whether she had even been inside them. She enquired where my school friends had come from, and envied any who were rich. She told me that rich people didn't live in their palaces all the time. When the weather is too hot and the air is close, they go off into the country where they have villas in the mountains or beside the sea.

This led us on to talk about the sea and I remarked that I knew several people who spent their summers at the seaside. She paused to listen and then asked me whether, when I was a man, I would take my children there. But I was not thinking of children, only of myself standing on some distant shore and the long way I should have to go to get there. Just at that moment we were walking past one of those massive garden doors and it so happened that the richest, rarest flowers became confused in my mind with the sea, so I found myself thinking of the windowbox filled with geraniums as though it was lying on the ocean floor.

Thus, riches, that my father slaved all day to acquire, seemed to me a fantasy. It took away my conviction that everybody coveted other people's possessions. I didn't understand their jealousy, nor, to tell the truth, what

it would be like to be rich. What seemed to me so exotic
was the idea that, beyond the horizon, there lay a promised
land where amazing things could happen. It made me
think of how I felt when a September moon was just
rising, though as yet it was still hidden by the trees. I
didn't understand what connection there could possibly be
between our harvests of grain and grapes and life in a
city, where there were such grand palaces. Sandiana,
walking around Bicocca estimating with a jaundiced
eye the yield we could expect from our harvest, dis-
couraged these ideas of mine. I wandered away, looking
for sloes.

Once, without telling me beforehand, she cleared a strip
of uncultivated land with the intention of planting corn
there. The work was done and the bushes cleared away
before I knew of it. I called her names, threatened her,
threw stones at her. She laughed. She didn't understand
my tears and so didn't say she was sorry. I kept on at
her so much that she lost her temper and complained to
my father, who beat me. Everybody grumbled at me all
the evening, because I didn't understand things. I wept
in secret and made up my mind to pay them out by not
looking at the hill beyond the geraniums for a long time.

But I watched it from the track through the reeds.
Merely being there made me feel alone. Even the distant
view, seen through the reeds, looked brighter and
more blue between the flowers and the sea. If I had
climbed a little higher — but I rarely went there now
and seldom alone — I could have seen the plain and the
little dots here and there that in reality were houses and
farms, almost lost in the mist. They might have been sails,
a little group of islands or patches of sea-foam. These
were the thoughts running through my head while I

spent the winter in town. Not that I talked about them to anyone. I proudly treasured them, deep down in my secret heart.

I would listen to the other boys talking and boasting, but I kept quiet, not because I wouldn't have enjoyed sharing my thoughts, but because by this time I had realised that things that are really true cannot be told. Not only is it essential that anyone listening should understand them, but he must also be prepared to understand them before he is told. In short it is impossible to learn truths from someone else. I used to ask myself about this when I began to understand such things, but it was as if these queries stemmed from the time when I learned to know my father.

One fine day Sandiana came to live with us and after a while I could hardly remember, nor could she, a time when she wasn't there.